Roger Munro

SHADOWS
AT SUNSET

TALES OF FEAR, FATE AND FOREBODING

To Jackie & John.

Best wishes

Roger

Roger Munro

SHADOWS AT SUNSET

TALES OF FEAR, FATE AND FOREBODING

MEREO
Cirencester

Mereo Books

1A The Wool Market Dyer Street Cirencester Gloucestershire GL7 2PR
An imprint of Memoirs Publishing www.mereobooks.com

Shadows at Sunset: 978-1-86151-415-8

First published in Great Britain in 2015
by Mereo Books, an imprint of Memoirs Publishing

The address for Memoirs Publishing Group Limited can be found at
www.memoirspublishing.com

The Memoirs Publishing Group Ltd Reg. No. 7834348

Cover design - Ray Lipscombe

The Memoirs Publishing Group supports both The Forest Stewardship Council® (FSC®) and
the PEFC® leading international forest-certification organisations. Our books carrying both the
FSC label and the PEFC® and are printed on FSC®-certified paper. FSC® is the only
forest-certification scheme supported by the leading environmental organisations including
Greenpeace. Our paper procurement policy can be found at
www.memoirspublishing.com/environment

Typeset in 12/18pt Bembo
by Wiltshire Associates Publisher Services Ltd. Printed and bound in Great Britain by
Printondemand-Worldwide, Peterborough PE2 6XD

CONTENTS

INTRODUCTION

"The oldest and strongest emotion of mankind is fear, and the oldest and strongest kind of fear is fear of the unknown." So said H P Lovecraft, an American author who achieved posthumous acclaim for his chilling works of dark fiction. Psychologists would have us believe that our fear of the unknown is a residue of traumatic events in our early lives that we haven't properly addressed and haven't managed to control because we instinctively run away, if we possibly can, from anything we regard as a threat to our well-being. Some of the stories in this book feature protagonists who are not in control of their own actions, as depicted in the stories *Caroline's Last Ride* and *Terminus*, or find it impossible to change course. Some of the characters would be free from danger if they could manage to get away *(Through the Eyes of Others)* or they are prevented from doing so by malevolent or sinister beings *(The Wind Farm)*. After all, our most feared demons are those which never go away, or even worse, those which keep coming back, as in *The Visitor*.

Dark fantasy is difficult to delineate but can best be translated as a metaphor for an effective means of bringing to our attention the fearful thoughts and memories we each have embedded deeply in our subconscious minds. Everything we experience in our lives affects us, if not consciously then subconsciously. We each of us therefore are strangely perturbed by things we cannot explain to ourselves, let alone to others, and what we as individuals find deeply disturbing may be of little or no concern to others. I remember as a child fearfully climbing the stairs in my grandparents' old house on the way to my bed, which was in a room at the end of a long, narrow corridor. Midway down the corridor was a room which was completely empty, the door of which was almost always closed. As a child, I wasn't disbarred from entering this room if I so wished, but for some inexplicable reason I was petrified of it and ran past the door each time I made my way down the corridor. Echoes of this trepidation are reflected in the story *Night Shift*. We all have dusty empty rooms, empty cobweb-strewn attics and dark empty cellars in the recesses of our minds.

The best and most convincing dark stories are succinct. They don't necessarily have substantive ghosts in them but their defining trait is that they provoke a psychological fear-response in the reader merely by suggesting that there is something present, so the reader may "feel" an entity brushing past them or sense that a seemingly ordinary person in their presence is anything but. Dark stories should disturb the thoughts of the reader to such an extent that they cannot differentiate between what is real and what is not, what has solidity rather than just being a shadow, and they can end up believing that their closest relative looks like an undertaker who knows he's going to get them in the end.

I hope you too will be disturbed by the stories in this book, which describe eerie and unfathomable events involving mortuaries, graveyards, unwelcome visitors and strange birds. When you read them, don't worry about the tapping on the window. Console yourself that any whispering you hear is probably just the wind. Be at peace when you read them - but try not to be alone when you do, since even death itself provides no safety.

To my grandchildren
Mia and Noam

THE FISHING MATCH

As Frank dozed half asleep in his warm bed, he was drifting in his dinghy through a vast shoal of feeding bass. Again and again the fish rolled and jumped, just begging to be offered a tasty, drifted sandeel. He didn't want to abandon his cosy sanctuary and his delightful dream, but the sound of branches pattering against the window increased until it sounded like sudden hail, and he could ignore it no longer.

He realised from the growing intensity of daylight that on this late December morning, it was high time he was up and dressed. It was the fishing club's last competition of the year that night, and he was determined to maintain the overall lead he had over his fellow members so that the coveted award for the 'Best Angler of the Year' would be his. After all, he deserved a day off after his hard work decorating the house. There were only the skirting boards left to gloss.

The setting for the competition was a spot on an island at the extreme tip of a remote peninsula in the far west of Wales; it would be an overnight contest. Mindful that he had but a brief window of time in which to cross the island's causeway - accessible only during low water - and anxious to arrive at his fishing mark before the early dusk of the winter's day, Frank dragged himself from his bed and began to gather his tackle together – rods, reels, lines, hooks, leads, bait and waterproofs. A quick glance at the weather forecast; fine for most of the day, but it seemed rain and strong winds would be coming in later. He fired up his ancient but trusted Ford and eagerly set off.

When Frank reached his destination that afternoon, it was still full daylight. However his growing excitement was tempered when he discovered that the only other car in the headland car park was a rusty and long-abandoned wreck. It seemed he had been in too much of a hurry; he was obviously the first.

Heavily laden with fishing gear and confident that his fellow club members would soon be hard on his heels, Frank set out along the narrow, beaten track which threaded its way across the peninsula. Away to the west the winter sun was beginning to slip down, a great golden ball. To the east, the sea and the sky had darkened to a leaden grey. The path took him through an expanse of quiet fields hemmed by lines of coal-black hedges against which the sheep scurried together under a huge brooding sky; the promised rain and storm clouds lowered over the distant, silent estuary. Beyond this, iron-grey marshes rippled in the dying light, shadow chasing gloomy shadow.

The path turned sharply to the north, running along the summit of the peninsula for about a mile before zigzagging downwards to the causeway. By the time Frank reached the island, the short winter's day was already closing in. He looked back the way he had come; there was no sign of his fellow anglers, or indeed of any other human being. Surveying the wide, mysterious vastness of the ocean all around him, he felt quite alone, and shivered as the evening shadows fell over him like a shroud. It seemed very strange that none of his friends had appeared. He hadn't bargained for quite this much solitude.

He began to pick his way gingerly down to the water's edge. At the point where a large, triangular stone capped the high cliff, he climbed down to a flat rocky platform near its base, raised a golden glow from his Tilly lamp, tackled up, cast out and started to fish, still in complete solitude. At least the conditions were promising; there ought to be a good chance of a codling or two, even a late-season bass.

But as the minutes and then the hours passed, the rod tip silhouetted against the almost-black winter sky remained obstinately untroubled by anything more interesting than the occasional lump of drifting bladderwrack. After several hours of fishing with no sound save the lapping of sea water, the moaning wind and the melancholy call of the gulls far out in the black void, Frank had failed to catch a single fish. And still he was alone.

It had now started to rain heavily, so he decided to move on to a more sheltered spot on the leeward side of the cliff face, just above the water line. As he rounded the next rocky protrusion he was surprised to see a figure standing at the edge of the ledge; a fellow angler, bathed in the dim, cold light of an old-fashioned lantern. Frank couldn't see how anyone could have passed him without being seen or heard, and there was no other way out to this spot. Very strange.

The man's head was covered by the hood of a grimy, grey foul-weather suit, so it was impossible to see who he was, or to confirm that it was one of his friends. He was standing motionless near the edge of the cliff, his rod beside him on a tripod, looking out over the dark ocean.

'Wouldn't like to fall in there,' said Frank jocularly to the figure. 'You'd never get out.'

The grey-suited figure turned very slowly to face him. In the dark Frank could not quite make out his face, except for two rows of broken, grinning teeth. Then something moved above the teeth, in the place where the man's left eye should have been. As the faint light caught the half-hidden face, Frank saw that it was a crab, crawling down from a gaping black eye socket.

The face was nothing more than a grinning skull.

'Ah, but I did,' hissed the corpse. 'And if it's fish you want, I can show them to you. Up close.' It raised a single skeletal hand and then swung it down, pointing down below the ledge to the swaying ocean below.

Frank started to back away in horror, but the figure was too quick for him. It took a single stride towards him, its creeping, sinuous fingers outstretched to seize him by the arm. Frank skidded on the wet rock, gasped in horror, and lost his balance. The two figures hit the water together.

The causeway would remain inaccessible for a few hours yet. Before long there would be two rusting, abandoned cars in the headland car park, and the unfinished skirting boards would have to be glossed by someone else.

DÉJÀ VU

The custodian of the ancient castle liked nothing better than to creep along the fringes of the crowded paths of life, warning all human kindness to keep its distance. He was as mean-spirited and bitter as the coldest winds of winter, unpredictable and prone to violent outbursts, as tough as steel and as solitary as the evening star. Although he hated all God's creatures with a vengeance, he particularly despised children, reserving for them a malice more venomous than that of a pit viper.

His grating voice reflected the cold within him, which shrivelled his skin and bent his wizened body like a shrunken mummy. His only joy in life was his beloved castle, which he had maintained for the last four decades with as much care and devotion as a mother would foster on her newborn child. The castle stood in secluded woodland which, towards the end of autumn, drew a thin grey cloud about its chill stones.

Isolated by the mist, the old man swept up the fallen leaves, stopping occasionally to look in irritation at the ever-growing pile. As he did so, at the edge of his visibility he noticed the castle's last remaining visitor of the day – a young boy of about eleven years old. To the custodian's horror, he was actually scratching his initials with a knife on the stonework of the walkway of a high parapet leading to the central turret.

Enraged that his cherished castle was being desecrated in such a casual manner, the custodian clambered up the turret's spiral stairway and confronted the young miscreant in fury.

'What do you think you're doing, you little vandal!' he bellowed. The boy just grinned back at him; he didn't even stop scratching.

'It's public property, I can do what I like and an old git like you ain't going to stop me' he replied.

The custodian let out a roar of exasperation and resentment. He strode up to the boy, who had clearly underestimated his adversary's speed and strength. His expression now changed to alarm and he turned to run; too late. The custodian pushed the boy away from his artwork with such force that the youngster lost his balance. Before the man could grab him, he toppled backwards over the parapet's rusticated masonry and dropped in silence through the void. There was a two-second pause, followed by a sickening thud as his small body struck the hard earthen floor of the castle keep, thirty feet below.

The custodian peered down. Even from this height it was clear, from the impossible angle of the boy's head, that he had broken his neck on impact.

Well, it served him right. That little swine had done unforgivable, irreparable damage to a 900-year-old castle. He had had it coming to him.

In the absence of any witness evidence, the Coroner recorded a verdict of accidental death. The old man smiled to himself at the news; he firmly believed the boy had got what he deserved. It wasn't as if he had caused the death of an innocent child. That little devil would only have gone on to worse crimes. His blubbing mother should be grateful that her young criminal had been taken off her hands sooner rather than later.

A year passed, and one autumn day as the light was fading, the old man crossed the castle courtyard again as it began to fill with twilight shadows. He heard the sinister, monotonous surging moan of the bleak wind, like the menacing whisper of a lost and despairing wanderer, and a shiver ran through him; he felt he was being watched.

He soon realised that this was indeed the case. On the high parapet, at the very point from which the boy had fallen twelve months before, he saw quite clearly the outline of a lonely figure.

He stared in disbelief. Impossible, but true - there, in silhouette against the darkening sky, stood the boy – the boy who had died at his hands this time last year. He remained motionless and said not a word, but his pale eyes seemed to stare down straight into the custodian's face.

The combination of the sudden appearance of the figure and the dreadfulness of its expression began to fill the custodian with fear and an apprehension of evil, driven by this apparition of a boy who he knew had been dead and buried twelve months since. The dreadful messenger of fate stared into the old man's conscience, whispering into the ear of his previously uncaring spirit. As they stared at each other the custodian could not take his eyes off the boy, who now slowly raised an arm and pointed accusingly at him. His face, dimly visible in the shadows, bore an expression of desperate malevolence, as though he was searching for something he wanted more than the life which had been taken from him.

Towards the old man who had taken that life, he now directed a blast of hatred and anger. The old man became confused, his heart beating wildly, gripped with acute fear. With the dreadful conviction of the reality that he had seen a creature of an unknown world and filled with terror by the apparition, he screamed out loud. His legs failed him and he swayed and fell, his head slowly drooping until his face rested in death on the leaves in which he lay.

The boy on the parapet was unaware of the terrible effect his appearance had had on the old man below. He let out a sigh of sadness and turned to plod wearily home. He was consoling himself with the knowledge that at last he had had the courage to visit the spot where his twin brother had lost his life so tragically, exactly one year before.

He had no idea that simply by appearing in exactly the right place at the right time, he had, quite unwittingly, avenged his brother's death.

CAROLINE'S LAST RIDE

Caroline's favourite route out of her village had always been the country road to the west. It might not have been as quick or easy as the motorway, but it took her out into quiet countryside and in no time at all she would find herself looking out over the vast open spaces of the rugged Atlantic shoreline. It was only when she could gaze upon this view that she felt completely free of the dreadful torment and the oppressive claustrophobia which had dogged her all her life. She had always been fearful of using elevators, of crowded places and of dark nights.

Sadly, in Caroline's busy life the opportunities for such ventures were quite rare, and she was able to make her escape no more than once or twice a year. She therefore looked forward to each pilgrimage with great longing.

The road west did however have one disadvantage; on her return journey she had to pass a particular spot on the dual carriageway which inexplicably filled her with dread each time she passed it. At the location in question, just off to the left of the main carriageway, she could see a winding road climbing up a steep hill which was topped by a small clump of Scots pines. Not once had she ever seen a person, a vehicle or indeed any living creature at all appear on this empty, desolate road, which was bordered on each side by dark, thorn-guarded hedgerows. The blackness of the hedges inflicted upon the lane a depressing and forbidding air, as though it was a passageway out of the natural world and into something darker and much less pleasant. Indeed, she regarded the road as the very embodiment of the road to hell. Each time she saw it on her return journey to the village, she experienced a heavy, ominous feeling, as if someone, or something, was watching her drive past. She was greatly relieved each time she saw that once again the road was empty, for she somehow knew that if she ever saw upon it either a vehicle or a person, it would be the portent of something terrible.

Following a seaside visit one late afternoon, Caroline passed the peculiar winding lane on the homeward journey as usual. She looked across at it – and found herself gripped by a sudden sense of dread and apprehension. For once, the lane was not empty. In the twilight gloom of the rain-swept sky she saw that a big black car had come to a dead stop near the summit of the hill.

For some reason, Caroline did not take the obvious course of accelerating away and leaving the scene safely behind her. Instead, confused and disorientated with fear, she pulled over to the side of the main carriageway, switched off the engine and gazed across at the scene.

As she watched, the driver's door of the big car opened and the figure of a man stepped out. He was a sallow, solitary figure, very tall and dressed very formally in black and wearing a top hat. He stepped towards her and as she watched, frozen in fear, he raised a gloved hand and beckoned her. He was clearly summoning her to cross the road and walk up the lane to join him. The man's face bore an expression of expectation and cold command which was dreadful to behold.

In her confused and terrified state, Caroline entirely forgot where she was. Overlooking the fact that she was on a busy main road, without taking her eyes off the man on the hill, she opened the door of her car and stepped out onto the roadway.

Barely had her foot made contact with the road when there was a blaring of horns and a screech of brakes as an articulated lorry roared down upon her, seemingly from nowhere. Instinctively she threw herself sideways behind her car and the huge truck skidded to one side, missing her by a hair's breadth.

Panting with shock, Caroline picked herself up and

rubbed the dust and gravel from her clothes. She realised that she had just escaped a quick but very messy death by a matter of inches. The truck had screeched to a halt a few yards further on. The cab window was wound furiously down and a tousled head appeared. The driver's face was red with anger.

'You were nearly bloody strawberry jam, lady!' he shouted. 'Good job I got good brakes on this thing!' He shook his head in disgust, wound the window back up and thundered off.

Caroline took several deep breaths in an effort to regain her composure. She knew how closely she had just escaped with her life.

As she went to open her car door to get back in and resume the journey home, she looked up at the strange winding lane to see that both the big black car and the solitary figure beside it had disappeared.

Curiously enough, Caroline never felt afraid after that when she drove, year after year, past the spot which had previously always filled her with such dread. Life for her became more peaceful and less troubled, and she maintained robust good health to a ripe old age.

But no one's health lasts for ever, and in her seventies Caroline began to suffer the intense, inescapable pain of acute arthritis. Ultimately the only relief was provided by regular treatment with large doses of morphine. Finally, one autumn day in her eightieth year, her heart gave out and she passed away.

On the day of her funeral a few days later, Caroline made her last journey along the western road from the village, but this time she did not continue along the main road to the coast; the route to the new cemetery took the cortege onto a side road and up the very hill which in life had once caused her such fear and dread. As the hearse approached the summit of the hill, its ancient engine began to stutter and die; its antiquated fuel pump was not at its best on slopes. The driver willed it on towards the top, but the engine died just too soon and the car rolled to a stop just below the summit. The driver, dressed smartly in the customary formal black clothing, got out of the car and slammed the door in exasperation.

Inside the heavy pine coffin, disturbed by the noise and vibration of the slammed door, Caroline's peaceful form stirred slightly, and her eyelids flickered.

The doctor who had certified death was young and inexperienced, and he had been on call for six nights running. Caroline was not dead, as he had assumed; she was in a deep, morphine-induced coma. Now the morphine was wearing off. And apart from the arthritis, there was very little wrong with her.

Caroline lay ruler straight, neatly arranged in her best dress as she had stipulated, in complete darkness inside the coffin, and now she was slowly beginning to come to. How dark it was, she thought; not at all like her bedroom, whose window faced east. Where on earth could she be? And now this strange, hard bed she was lying on was somehow being lifted up, and then gently lowered again. And it was so very stuffy in here. What could possibly be going on?

Very faintly she could hear a man's voice, solemn and slow, almost as if somewhere in the distance, someone was holding a church service. In fact it sounded very much like her own vicar, dear old Tom Peabody, but clearly that was impossible.

Now something was landing noisily on the ceiling close above her; rain? Hail? But not in September, surely? This was all rather worrying. She felt very weak. She tried to lift a hand to explore, but it immediately encountered a hard, solid surface, barely inches above her head.

Caroline let out a muffled scream of terror, but it was hopelessly drowned out by the thunder of soft Somerset loam, a wheelbarrow full of it this time, as it cascaded down on to the coffin.

Above ground, beside the grave, The Reverend Peabody clapped his bible shut.

'Caroline was truly a credit to this community and this parish' he murmured reassuringly to the little knot of remaining mourners. 'Now that she has left us for a better world, we must all take comfort from the dignity and composure with which she spent her final days. Even through her pain, not a word of complaint was heard to pass her lips. Caroline is now happy and safe with her maker. Long may she rest in peace.'

NIGHT SHIFT

It was the darkest of November nights, and Reginald Norman Lumley, midway through his night shift at the council offices, felt full of resentment that most of the rest of humanity had already been slumbering in their warm and comfortable beds for a good few hours. Despite his best endeavours at staying awake, Reg was beginning to grow sleepy himself, for there was something unendurably tedious about trying to stay awake listening to the dismal, ceaseless moaning of the wind whistling through the window cracks. He hated the long overnight shifts he had to endure as watchman of the sprawling municipal building, which bore as much evidence of decay and age as did Reg himself. It did not help that at the far end of the long corridor which housed his dingy, cheerless office was the public mortuary. The one bright spot on the horizon was Reg's impending retirement, now just a few weeks away.

The long hours passed as slowly as they always did on a night shift. Although Reg moved from chair to chair in an attempt to stay awake and even tried rereading his *Daily Mail* a couple of times, his state of melancholy depression was not helping, and eventually he drifted into a restless and fitful slumber. He began to dream of an endless procession of dead souls sweeping past him on the wind, vainly trying to arrest their flight in order to bring themselves back to the world of the living. Their bodies seemed to be fabricated from an amalgam of various nameless organs dissected during their autopsies, all of course performed in the mortuary at the end of the corridor.

It was a noise rather than this distasteful dream that eventually awoke Reg from his slumber; the distant sound of the fire alarm. He ignored it, for he was suddenly convinced that he was not alone. Was it his imagination, or could he hear from along the passage muffled footfalls and distant talking voices, strange cries as of lost and despairing wanderers? He waited for the noises to crystallise into something more identifiable, something that would allow him to shrug off his fears and settle back to sleep, but the more he listened, the stranger the noises grew. Gradually his puzzlement turned to dismay and his dismay to fear and dread. The sounds were inexplicable and other-worldly.

Battling to control his rising panic, Reg rose from his chair, pushed open the door with sweating fingers and charged out into the long, dimly-lit corridor, turning left, away from the mortuary and towards the safety of the exit door at the far end. As he rushed down the narrow corridor he hesitated, heart thumping even harder, for now he could hear a swift, peculiar creaking tread coming from something immediately behind him.

With a dreadful reluctance he stopped and looked back. Surely, surely he was imagining it?

But he was not. As he looked round, he found himself staring at a human figure enveloped in what appeared to be a shroud-like garment and framed by dim shadows. There was sufficient light for him to see that its face bore a look of terror, and its hollow, staring eyes seemed to belong to someone who was already destined for the grave. Surely it was his own face – corpse-like, lost to the living but still, somehow, the face of Reginald Norman Lumley, night watchman?

The figure spoke not a word; it could only gape back at Reg as Reg gaped at it. He was surely witnessing a vision of his own death. His heart beat wildly, stricken with terror, and he turned and rushed headlong through the exit door.

It was the cleaners who found Reg lying in a heap at the foot of the stairwell early the next morning, his eyes staring wide in death. No one could ever work out what had brought on his apparent heart attack, or what he had been doing trying to leave the building without his coat, his torch, his sandwich box and his newspaper. It did not occur to the investigating police officers that the fire alarm had caused the fire door halfway along the corridor to creak shut automatically behind Reg as he fled, dimly showing him his own reflection in the glass when he turned. The verdict, presumably, would be natural causes; but first, the late Reginald Norman Lumley had an appointment with the mortuary.

FOLLOW MY LEADER

It was a golden late summer's day, the kind which made one glad to be alive. The small group of six cyclists had spent the morning riding at a leisurely pace through deep, green countryside along narrow lanes lined with butter-yellow cornfields under enormous cloudless skies. By midday they had reached a pretty seaside village peppered with freshly painted, pastel-coloured cottages, each with window boxes full of geraniums and gardens brimming with wild flowers and herbs.

The riders were delighted to discover that the village had a quaint little tea-room where they spent a pleasant half hour enjoying cups of tea, delicious chocolate cake and little sugar pastries. Good-natured wayfarers bade them good day or stopped to say nice things about their bicycles whilst they sat and admired the sun dancing over the crystal clear surface of the azure sea.

The six had enjoyed many such days since they had all retired from their busy careers. One of the most enjoyable features of each day's ride was that they all took turns at being the lead rider, whose decision it was to determine the day's route and choose a 'secret' destination before returning home. John, the oldest member, and his wife Val were retired teachers, whereas the other married couple, Gwyn and Linda, had been senior partners in a large and thriving law firm. All four had done their best to bring together the two single members of the group, Luke and Catherine, but had failed to do so despite persistent and heartfelt efforts. Catherine, a pretty, bright-eyed, vivacious ex-nurse, seemed keen enough on the handsome Luke, but he always appeared somewhat moody and withdrawn. He seemed to live much of the time in the past and showed little interest in any new relationships, although he was always polite and considerate and enthusiastically joined in the group's activities. Today Luke was lead rider, so he had the challenging task of getting everyone out of their comfortable tea-room chairs and back onto their machines for the afternoon ride.

In single file they tackled the precipitous lanes which climbed slowly up from the sea, while songbirds called and whistled cheerily from thick orchards on both sides of the road. Although they appeared to be winding their way into deep countryside, they could tell they had not left the sea far behind; the crying of gulls up in the hot blue sky was a constant reminder.

Gradually the coast road levelled out, and soon the little party were enjoying spectacular views of the ocean far below. Eventually, as the sun began to sink towards the far-off western horizon, they took the opportunity to stop at a roadside café to admire the sea-views and enjoy some fish and chips wrapped in vinegary newspaper. There was much chatter about the events of the day. Only Luke did not seem to have much to say.

'What's the matter, still worried about that derailleur?' said Gwyn, trying to provoke Luke, who could be slightly obsessive about the correct functioning of his machine, into conversation with a little well-intentioned teasing. 'I'd stick a bit of gaffer tape round it if I were you.'

'Come on Luke, we're playing confessions' said Val. 'You've got to tell us something no one else knows about you.'

'Yeah, he was 18 before his mum took his stabilisers off his bike' put in John.

'Nasty! Look, why don't you tell us a bit more about that race you did in Corsica?'

'I've told you' said Luke. 'There's not much to add really. It was very hot and I won because most of the rest of them got heat exhaustion.'

'So where are you taking us then, Luke?' asked Catherine. 'What's the secret destination? It can't be much further, surely.'

'Probably a computer superstore' said Gwyn. 'Better hurry, they close at eight.'

'Talking about that, we really ought to get going' said Luke, ignoring the jibe. 'The light's beginning to go. The final bit is quite steep and narrow, but you'll be OK, just make sure you follow me. Don't let your pace drop, because after the downhill bit there's quite a steep climb. But it's heavenly when you get there, you'll see.' He gave one of his rare smiles.

Luke straddled his expensive machine and led the group off. After a few miles he turned down a side lane, apparently leading them back towards the sea. The rush of cool evening air on the riders' sunburned skin was refreshing and exhilarating.

Finally, quickly looking back to make sure they were all still following, Luke turned into a narrow unmade trackway.

'Come on, nearly there now' he called.

One by the one the other five riders followed him. They now found themselves riding down a deep sunken path between tall hedges. The light here was very poor, and each of them was glad of the bright clothing of the rider in front.

Gwyn was the second rider, immediately behind Luke. Suddenly the path took a sharp right turn, and Luke in front seemed to accelerate away and flash out of sight.

Anxious to make sure he did not lose him, Gwyn skidded round the corner as fast as he dared, the others hard on his heels.

Gwyn rounded the bend to take in two things simultaneously; Luke standing beside his machine at the side of the track with a wide grin on his face, and a gaping blue void in front where the track should have continued. It was far too late now for Gwyn to stop or change course. There was a second of furious, futile braking as his tyres scrabbled for grip in the dust, and then with a horrible shock, he found himself flying over the cliff edge and riding silently out into empty space.

The last thing he saw before he hit the rocks three hundred feet below was his wife's bright yellow bicycle as it overtook him on its separate way to destruction.

The following morning at low water, five broken bodies and five expensive, but equally broken, touring bicycles were recovered from the rocks.

No one ever found out what had happened to Luke. In fact, far away in another town, he was already beginning to miss his cycling trips with his friends. Time to put another ad in the local paper.

'Retired professional seeks fellow cycling enthusiasts to form a small group. Let's have fun and keep fit together. Call me on the following number…'

RHYME AND REASON

Jack Horner was sitting in a corner seat in his favourite village inn. It was the week before Christmas, and he was enjoying a well-deserved pint of ale and a fruit pie filled with plums.

'Hey, Horner,' shouted the landlord, 'if you have to pick those plums from your pie then for God's sake use a spoon instead of your dirty fingers!'

But Jack couldn't help himself – he was absolutely ravenous and the pie was delicious, particularly the pastry, which was the best he'd ever tasted. The landlord bought his pies from Mr Crumb, the village baker.

Miffed at being scolded by the landlord, Jack left the inn feeling rather disappointed at the lack of any opportunity to gorge himself on a second plum-filled pie. Once he got outside his mood became even darker, for much to his annoyance, he bumped headlong into George

Porgie, an old school acquaintance, who was running like the wind along the pavement.

'Mind where you're going Georgie!' shouted Jack.

Heavily burdened by a hefty pudding of his own and an equally large pie, George stopped for breath. He was reasonably satisfied that he had at last eluded a gang of boys who were hell-bent on getting their hands on him. George's mouth was heavily covered with red, and Jack assumed it was the juice of all the plums he had eaten.

'What's up Georgie?' asked Jack hopefully. 'That's a nice looking pie you've got there, is it plum?'

'It's steak and kidney, if you must know,' replied George, rather defensively. 'I bought it from the pie stall in the village fair. I had to wait ages for some kid called Simon who was buying a pie at the same time, but he just couldn't count out his change properly. A fellow called Johnny told me he had been waiting absolutely ages to get served too. I've tried a piece of the pie and the pastry's luscious. The pie man told me he gets his pies from Mr. Crumb in the village. I've never seen anyone gobble a pie as quickly as that boy Simon did – it must have been the lovely pastry!'

Still feeling disgruntled at the lost opportunity of another plum pie, Jack decided to call in the bakery on his way home to buy a couple of plum pies directly from Mr. Crumb. The old baker's pies were famous for miles around. His current batch were even better than usual, so much so that the owner of the local aviary placed a large order with Mr Crumb because he was convinced that his birds thrived on them – particularly the blackbirds, of which he had a couple of dozen.

When Jack eventually arrived at the bakery the air was thick with clouds of fluffy flour, and the smell of newly-baked produce was mouth-watering. Mr Crumb's hat was dusted with flour and his apron was spattered all over with egg. Jack could feel the heat from the big brick oven and see the gleaming rows of bakery pans. Mr. Crumb was as busy as ever, and as Jack walked in he was finishing off an Easter pie for old man Tuffet's daughter, who apparently liked it made with ricotta prepared from curds and whey mixed with plenty of egg.

'Afternoon Jack,' said Mr Crumb. 'For one minute there I thought you were that Hubbard woman scrounging for bread again. What can I do for you?'

'I'd like a couple of your delectable plum pies please, Mr Crumb. They really are scrumptious, have you got a secret recipe or what?'

Mr. Crumb smiled, winked at Jack and said, 'It's all in the eggs I use for the puff pastry lad. It's all in the eggs!'

Just then a mouse ran up the old clock behind the counter in the bakery. The clock struck one and the mouse ran down again just as a large, obese woman rushed into the bakery.

'Have any of you seen my boy?' she asked in desperation. 'I've been told he's had a nasty fall but I don't know where he is.'

Mr Crumb hesitated for a moment, then rather sheepishly said, 'He could be anywhere by now Mrs Dumpty – he could be here, there and everywhere. Would you like to take a pie home with you? Or maybe not.'

SHADOWS AT SUNSET

The evening was particularly lovely, even for a fine autumnal day reaching its peaceful, glorious end. A delicate veil of blue mist spread over the distant hills, and golden sunshine was softly stealing over the sweet, mild evening air, which was tinged with the faint sense of melancholy appropriate to a mellow, sunny late autumn afternoon.

The dead leaves and occasional chestnuts that covered the ground slipped away silently in the gentle wind as Winnie Overfield made her way up the hill on her return from her long daily walk. The cottage in which she lived, alongside the cottage on the opposite side of the lane, stood like lonely sentinels on the edge of the village, as if guarding entry to the settlement beyond.

Buried within the leafless trees of the nearby woods, the clock tower struck four, its sound harping down the wind as Winnie wearily reached her front garden gate. She noticed the long, golden rays of the setting sun shining brightly on the opposite cottage, whose tall, wide window-panes were glowing like fires.

The drawn curtains on the upper windows had remained closed for years, ever since the death of the old widower who had lived there all alone. But the curtains on the ground floor were fully open, so at this moment the low, broad streaming rays of the dying sun allowed the woman to see directly into the sitting room of the long-empty cottage.

Something of the atmosphere of an oratory was imparted to the empty sitting room, because on its back wall directly behind the staircase was the shadowy form of what appeared to be a tall crucifix, but which in reality was no more than a piece of broken fencing in the front garden.

The short day drew in and began to fill with lengthening shadows. The crisp brown leaves which littered the front garden smelled of fungus and rotting vegetation. Now, stirred by the faint breeze, they began a macabre dance. A sudden gust of wind set the leafless branches of the trees behind the empty cottage in motion, making them appear to Winnie like the flailing arms of someone who was struggling to escape from some kind of evil trance.

Winnie looked into the house, and was frozen in horror. There inside was a dark shadow which appeared to be human in form. As she watched transfixed, it rose to a standing posture beside the tall crucifix and then slowly began to ascend, as if climbing the stairs.

Dark cloud now veiled the sun, and the twilight took on an eerie purple glow. The trees seemed to pause as if waiting for something. Winnie thought she heard a taunting whisper carried on the mournful wind – *'we always come, just as we always do.'*

She looked behind her, but there was nothing there. She hurried inside her cottage and locked the door, glad to get away from the chilly evening air and whatever else might be mingled within the beckoning shadows of the closing day.

The fine autumnal weather continued the next morning. On the afternoon of the following day, having dismissed her unsettling experience of the previous evening as a mere figment of her imagination, Winnie set off again for her usual walk. And once again, just as the village clock struck four, there was the dark shadow climbing the stairway of the empty cottage.

Never again did Winnie venture to go walking in that wood on her own. Bewildered and frightened by what she had experienced, she became increasingly anxious and longed for some kind of explanation.

Finally she asked her husband Jack how long the old man in the cottage across the lane had been dead.

'Must be at least ten years this month,' he replied. 'He

was just like you, a creature of habit. He had his set routine and went up to bed every day without fail for his afternoon nap. I can't remember whether it was at four o'clock or five.'

'It was four,' murmured Winnie. She spoke with absolute certainty.

Unable to overcome the distress and shock of the ordeal she had experienced, Winnie was herself dead within a matter of months. At four o'clock on fine autumnal afternoons a shadow climbs the hill which leads to the village. God help anyone who sees it if they also hear the wind whisper, *we always come, just as we always do.*

PRACTICE MAKES PERFECT

Rebecca's favourite book as a child had been *The Lord of the Rings*, and her most admired character was Legolas the Sindar Elf, a master archer with keen eyesight, sensitive hearing and excellent bowmanship. Legolas' exploits inspired her, at the tender age of nine, to take up archery. She tried it first at a local club where her grandfather had been a lifelong member, then joined a bigger club where many of the members were competitors in national and international competitions.

Rebecca's skill grew, and she soon became so obsessed with archery that she could never entirely stop thinking about it, even when she was in school or out shopping with her parents. Fortunately both of them were supportive and understood what was required from their child to progress in her chosen sport.

Rebecca was not a naturally gifted archer, but her

abundant personal attributes more than made up for this deficiency. She had an excellent ability to concentrate and was always willing to listen to her coach. She had the ability to follow instructions and to do what she was asked instantly without question. She was also totally dedicated to the sport and always practised, even during the cold winter months, shooting arrows in her garden or at the city's indoor archery range after school.

Every day involved four to five hours of shooting practice, then a five-mile run followed by a further two hours of strength and conditioning in the gym so that her heart rate wouldn't rise under stressful conditions; this helped her to control her shots.

When she saw a flaming arrow ignite the torch at the opening ceremony of the 1992 Olympic Games, there was only one thing on her mind. Getting through to the next Olympic finals wasn't going to be enough – she had to win the individual gold, no matter what the cost. Through sheer determination and devotion to her sport, Rebecca managed to gain admission to the junior Olympic archery development programme, and subsequently became successful at senior level in the individual District, Regional and National Target Championships and the National Masters Tournament.

She was meticulous about the quality of her arrows, the tuning of her bow and the guaranteed availability of spare parts. She became so obsessed that her coach and parents started to worry about her mental state. She had neither a social life nor friends. The only relatively close contact she had was with Stella, a fellow competitor in the national archery female squad. She took a keen interest in Stella, because she regarded this naturally-gifted archer as a real threat to her own selection for the one available place in the national Olympic team as its representative in the individual archery competition.

Rebecca had always had to work hard at mastering her sport, so she understandably resented Stella's laid-back approach, her natural strength, good temperament, steady hand, keen eye and ability to keep calm. But most of all she resented the fact that Stella never seemed to focus on the job at hand. She rarely attended competitions and hardly ever practised, because she was so naturally talented that she didn't really need to.

Rebecca grew more anxious, and as the selection day for the Olympic squad grew nearer she struggled to maintain her composure. She became intensely irritated when she realised that Stella was not in the least bit bothered.

On the morning of the elite competition which would ultimately dictate squad selection, both girls undertook a final practice round together in the High Performance Centre before anyone else arrived. Considering the stress she was under, Rebecca scored reasonably well with her first six arrows, but she realised that the writing was on the wall when Stella subsequently achieved a perfect score.

'Well done' said Rebecca, through gritted teeth.

'Oh that's nothing, I did it three times yesterday' said Stella, and she marched off up the field to retrieve her arrows from the target.

There is no sound when an arrow is fired. As Stella looked back towards the stand, she just had time to gape in horror as the arrow left Rebecca's bow. A second later, it had penetrated her body from breast to backbone and skewered her neatly to the bull's eye. Stella slumped downwards, eyes staring, her lifeless body pinned to the target by the single arrow, its bright red feathers sparkling in the sun.

That was the problem with having so much competition, reflected Rebecca. It was all very well being a natural athlete, but to come first - well, you really had to have the killer instinct.

THE VISITOR

Throughout the day a prolonged, gentle sprinkle of snow had wafted down over the silent neighbourhood, so that by evening the entire area was covered with a thick white blanket which enhanced the stillness of the midwinter dusk. By midnight, the snow had stopped and the sky was clearer than it had been for several nights. The air was crisp and cold, and from high above the moon shone down on the ranks of white and frozen trees.

Although the air was soft, there was a sound in it as of the breath of a sleeper awakening from a dark and disturbing dream. Tom Goodwright, who lived in the last terraced house at the edge of the village had gone to bed with a heavy heart. He was worrying about his elderly father, with whom he shared the house and for whom he had cared throughout his adult life. The old man had fallen foul of a flu virus which had recently taken many lives in the neighbourhood, and he was ailing and very weak.

It must have been a good deal later when Tom was awakened by the queer feeling that there was something present that hadn't been there when he had drifted off. Unable to get back to sleep, he arose from his bed, sat in a chair by the window and gazed out into the night.

The gentlest of breezes was now stirring the night air; it was no more than enough to make a faint sighing sound in the branches. In Tom's troubled mind strange voices seemed to be weeping in the trees, like heralds of foreboding.

And then he was suddenly conscious of something else. Someone was standing at the front gate of his neighbour's garden, a dark figure in the glimmer of the lamplight. He began to feel very uncomfortable. Yet despite a creeping and disagreeable sensation, he felt an overwhelming urge to look; he could not help himself.

The arrival of the intruder had left not a trace of any footprints or imperfections in the snow which had been so perfectly laid by nature. Perhaps it was not a human figure at all, but just his imagination playing tricks.

Tom observed with a sort of involuntary precision that the figure had a very noticeable twist of its head, so that it appeared to be looking directly at his neighbour's house. It had no face. It was a snowman which had only one arm, formed from a thorny tree-branch with which it appeared to beckon Tom's neighbour.

Convinced that the interruption to his sleep was playing tricks with his imagination, Tom went back to bed and spent a restless night whilst his mind tried to make sense of what he had seen.

The following morning, the news that his neighbour had died during the night from what appeared to be the effects of flu came as no great surprise. He was, after all, just one more victim of the virus which had killed so many of the villagers.

Despite his weariness after the interrupted sleep of the previous night, Tom retired late to bed. He had had to sit up most of the evening with his father, whose deteriorating health was causing him increasing concern. Finally, exhausted and beginning to feel the onset of flu symptoms himself, he plodded up to his room and went across to draw his curtains. As he did so he looked out of the window – and did a double take. Surely that could not be his father walking large as life down the garden path towards the front gate? And there once again at the gate stood that peculiar snowman! The rotted fallen leaves in the place where its face should have been seemed to form a skewed, sly smile.

He pulled the curtains firmly shut and tucked himself in, and eventually he managed to calm his troubled mind and fall into a deep slumber.

It was not until the following morning that light

dawned on Tom, in more senses than one. When he went down to see to his father, he found him lying cold and lifeless in his bed. Suddenly, he knew what it all meant. He understood with a terrible certainty that the snowman was no innocent edifice of snow, but a harbinger of death.

Tom's attention was taken up during the rest of the day with making the funeral arrangements and contacting his father's few relatives and friends. He could have done without it, particularly as the flu, or whatever it was, had now taken a firm grip and was making him feel very unwell indeed. Once again, it was late before, finally alone in the house which was now his own property, he managed to trudge wearily up the stairs to his room.

As he reached for the curtains, he froze in his tracks. There at the gate, once again, was the snowman. As usual, he could discern no features on the face of the creature, but he had the distinct impression that it was watching him with a fixed and malevolent glare.

Hurriedly, Tom drew the curtains. He was damned if some stupid snowman was going to keep him awake. Surely it had got what it wanted?

He decided to try to look on the bright side. Although he had yet to bury his father, it had occurred to him that he was now free to do all the things he had always wanted to accomplish; travel, adventure, perhaps even a little romance. After all, he was not yet fifty years old.

Happily making plans for a future of freedom, Tom drifted off to sleep. Outside, the snowman continued to watch and to wait. The collector of souls had all the time in the world.

FRIENDS FOR LIFE

The two elderly widows had lived for several years as neighbours in thatched, semi-detached cottages right in the heart of the village. Mary, the older of the two, had lost her husband under unexplained circumstances during the Second World War, while Daphne's partner had died from blood poisoning apparently caused by an animal or insect bite.

Although the two had become firm friends and shared most of their daily experiences, their personalities and appearances were quite different. Mary was a somewhat dowdy figure who made little attempt to look smart, even when they went shopping to the nearest town together, or attended formal events. She never bothered with make-up, never wore jewellery and her clothes appeared to be randomly selected with little thought to colour co-ordination. Daphne, on the other hand, was always immaculately turned out. She dressed in fashionable, expensive clothes and wore fine jewellery. She favoured black dresses or suits, of which she had many, and with which she always wore a necklace bearing a large deep-green diamond which matched her unusually large green eyes.

Whereas Mary appeared a little dim and somewhat slow at appreciating her surroundings, Daphne was well educated and had an impressive knowledge of most worldly events and places, a reflection of the fact that she had travelled widely before settling in the village. Daphne had no family, so Mary, who had two daughters and five grandchildren, took great delight in sharing with her the ups and downs of the lives of her relatives, none of whom Daphne had ever met.

Mary loved cooking and frequently prepared sumptuous meals which she enthusiastically shared with Daphne, while Daphne was only too glad of the opportunity to enjoy her neighbour's hospitality. They led idyllic lives surrounded by beautiful countryside which afforded them the opportunity of taking long leisurely walks, during which they both took a keen interest in the flora and fauna of the neighbourhood. They were both active members of the local Women's Institute, they both sang in the church choir and both sat on the committee of the district cottage hospital. Mary liked nothing better than preparing a wide selection of home-cooked jams, cakes, meat pies and a variety of quiches for the village summer fete and mince pies, puddings and game pie for the Christmas fair. Daphne was very happy to help Mary by doing all the shopping for her, since she particularly enjoyed the walk down to the grocer's shop and spending time chatting in the butcher's at the far end of the village. The only discernible area of difference between the pair was Mary's propensity to retire early and rise in the late morning, whereas Daphne hardly slept at all.

As time passed the two women grew closer and closer. They came to enjoy each other's company so much that neither ventured anywhere without the other, and they provided each other with as much mutual support as was required in times of need. Neither of them felt the need to spend time with anyone else, and in fact as time went on they began to resent any intrusion by any outsider, a definition which eventually included Mary's relatives.

And so life for the two of them went on from one blissful day to the next, until one year in the week running up to Christmas, Mary answered the door to a complete stranger who introduced herself as her new next-door neighbour. Convinced that the woman was completely mistaken, but nevertheless a little confused, Mary explained that she already had a long-standing neighbour of many years - Daphne.

Just then, Mary noticed that behind her visitor a large

black dog was advancing slowly up her neighbour's garden path. Around its neck was a black leather collar, and attached to the collar was a large, deep-green diamond which appeared to be the exact double of the gem worn by Daphne in her necklace.

The dog stopped and turned to look at Mary. There was something very strange about its eyes. Every Labrador Mary had ever seen had had deep brown eyes. This one had green eyes; Daphne's eyes.

The dog snarled menacingly, saliva drooling from its mouth. Then it turned to walk away.

Mary knew that one day it would be back. And then she remembered with horror how she had observed, with a mixture of disgust and puzzlement, the way Daphne enthusiastically licked her dinner plate.

TERMINUS

It was late on a warm summer's evening, and a fresh cool wind was blowing into the dusty city streets. It was almost as if nature itself was signalling a change in the air, and it made Ronnie Sharp feel uneasy, although he could not be sure exactly why. After all was said and done he'd had a good day – in fact, a very good day indeed. What's more, he was determined that what remained of it would be even better.

This was because Ronnie had spent most of the morning robbing the innocent tourists who were milling around the city's iconic landmarks. Well satisfied with his haul, he was now planning to spend the afternoon fleecing his fellow passengers on one of the tourist buses which operated on a circular route linking the city's most frequented venues. He'd always found the tourists to be an easy target, since they were invariably preoccupied with lapping up the sights and sounds which the city had to offer, and this usually made them completely oblivious to the fact that they were being relieved of their possessions by a skilled and unscrupulous villain.

Ronnie was cunning and manipulative. He was incapable of feeling empathy, guilt or remorse for his many nefarious deeds, which had included the brutal killing of an elderly couple during a robbery in their own home and the ruthless murder of his own mother so that he could inherit what little money she possessed in her meagre estate.

Thankfully, Ronnie didn't have to wait long at the bus stop before the elongated, crimson coloured bendy-bus came inching slowly up the road and its hydraulic doors opened with a hiss to welcome him into its embrace. With growing anticipation of the easy pickings which awaited him, he wandered down the aisle of the bus and took a seat next to a window right at the back of the rear compartment, so that he could observe all the unsuspecting passengers. The vehicle shuddered back into life, pulling away from the pavement as the doors sealed shut before stumbling onto the next leg of its circuitous journey. With each turn of a corner the bus juddered from side to side.

The rather dim fluorescent lights inside the bus provided just enough illumination for Ronnie to see that there were only three passengers seated in the front compartment, which was separated by a glass door from the rear compartment, while in the rear there was only one other passenger apart from himself, a large man. The driver remained obscured.

At the first stop, an even-toned voice announced: 'Tower of London. Will disembarking passengers please ensure they have their entry tickets ready.' A man and a woman from the front compartment disembarked. Ronnie had decided to follow them, but for some reason he found he could not get his seat belt unfastened. He struggled furiously with it, but now the bus was moving off again. Cursing, he sat back in his seat.

As the bus pulled away, he saw that the couple who had just got off the bus were walking back past it along the pavement. They could obviously see him too, for now they looked directly at him through the glass, nodding their heads in recognition and smiling. With a jolt, Ronnie realised that he knew them. And yet – it was impossible! They looked just like the elderly couple he had despatched in their own home, when they had been foolish enough to try to stop him taking their bits of useless jewellery.

At the next stop, the voice intoned, 'Madame Tussaud's. Will disembarking passengers please ensure they have their entry tickets ready.' The elderly lady who was the last passenger in the front compartment got to her feet and made for the exit. Ronnie decided he would follow her instead, but yet again his seat belt would not let him.

As the bus pulled away, he looked at the woman who

had just left the bus – and had an even greater shock. It was none other than his dead mother, or her spitting image. She stood on the pavement, pointing a finger at him and smiling a most knowing smile.

Ronnie was now shaking with fright. What was going on?

Except for the man who remained in the rear compartment, the bus was now empty. He focused his attention on his sole remaining fellow passenger. His head was bowed as if he was staring at the ground, but his features were obscured by the high collar of an old-fashioned overcoat and the rim of a dark grey military cap, despite the warmth of the summer's night.

But now Ronnie was distracted from his inspection and his alarm increased, for the bus was quite definitely going the wrong way. It appeared to be following a tortuous detour away from the main tourist areas into the dingy, dimly-lit streets of one of the city's less salubrious quarters.

Finally the bus stopped, and Ronnie heard the voice say, 'This bus terminates here. All remaining passengers must disembark.'

Ronnie reached for the recalcitrant seat belt again, and this time he found to his relief that it had unlocked itself. The tall man on his left stood up to leave, and turned to Ronnie with a cold grin. He was clad in a heavy grey military uniform and was wearing a German Iron Cross and swastika. What was going on? Was he going to a fancy dress party? Yet it would have been hard to imagine anyone who looked as if he was less out for fun.

Ronnie followed the man warily out, but as he alighted from the bus the man suddenly whirled round and gripped his arm with a hand of steel.

'Let go!' what do you think you're doing?' squealed Ronnie. But the man's grip simply tightened. He grinned, raised his free hand and pointed wordlessly to the entrance of the building opposite the place where the bus had stopped. Ronnie looked in bewilderment.

On each side of the entrance were massive pillars, connected by an overarching illuminated sign. In blood-red letters it read: 'The Gates of Hell'. Underneath, a smaller sign read: 'No entry ticket required.'

A LESSON FROM GRANDMA

Nathan was just 12 years old when his parents were killed in a road traffic accident involving a driver laden with drink and drugs. His only surviving relative was his housebound maternal grandmother who, despite her advanced age, felt duty bound to become his legal guardian. A lifelong and very keen gardener and horticulturist, she had always adored children and was devoted to Nathan, but as he grew older he showed her less and less respect and ceased to appreciate anything she did for him.

Nathan had grown tall and slim by the time he reached his late teens, but by no means healthy. He was always shabbily dressed in a grimy T-shirt, tracksuit trousers and dirty trainers and invariably had a fake gold chain around his neck. Despite being unemployed, he somehow managed to acquire everything he needed in the way of modern gadgets and never seemed short of money. He led a chaotic, drug-filled life-style and laughed at the idea that he might attend a rehab clinic. His grandmother had suspected for a long time that he was involved with drugs but she never mentioned it, mainly because her grandson ignored her and hardly ever engaged her in conversation except to ask whether anyone had left any telephone messages for him, or to scrounge money from her.

The old woman's suspicions were reinforced one morning when the police called at the house to search the property and enquired as to the whereabouts of her grandson, whom she hadn't seen for several days. He eventually turned up, but paid scant regard to his grandmother, as usual. He had two mobile phones on him, and as soon as he arrived home one of them rang. He spoke quickly – 'You want twenty bags of cocaine dubs and four of H?' – then went straight back out again.

Having made a lot of money from selling drugs, Nathan had moved up the ladder to become top boy. He was bulk-buying drugs from aggressive street dealers, all of which he then supplied and peddled to vulnerable schoolchildren and young adults. His increasingly infirm grandmother felt powerless to do anything about it. She spent all her time rocking gently back and forth in her beloved, highly-polished rocking chair with her trusty black hardwood walking cane hooked around its arm. Her only pleasure came from reading, and her favourite volume was a large, black-leather-bound encyclopaedia of gardening which had a beautiful golden calligraphic typeface and armoured ornamented bindings with heavy metalwork at the corners with clasps and latches that held it shut.

Her wise old eyes often brimmed with tears over her loneliness and the growing anger she felt towards her grandson's contemptuous behaviour. She sat before the fire alone with her thoughts, trying to recall the more gentle memories of her earlier life. She usually set freshly-cut logs on her fireplace to induce a slow aromatic burning, and while the firelight brought a blush to her cheeks she would remember the love and affection she had shared with the children she had taught in her earlier life as a teacher of botany. The anguish of loneliness and the pain she felt at the damage her grandson was relentlessly inflicting on countless young victims led to a heartache which finally killed her.

Nathan hardly missed a beat when the old woman finally passed away. He didn't even bother to attend her funeral. The only positive action he took was to increase the available space in the house for his growing stash of drugs by shoving the old woman's rocking chair into a corner of the sitting room and tossing her beloved books onto a high shelf, to put them as out of his way as possible.

The night following his grandmother's funeral, he

arrived home just before midnight high on heroin and drink with the sole intention of picking up a large bundle of drugs destined for certain naïve members of the local youth club. He was profoundly irritated to find that the electricity supplied had been cut off because the bill hadn't been paid.

Nathan began to feel distinctly uneasy in the darkness. Moonlight flooded the living room with eerie white light, and black shadows lay sharp-edged behind every piece of furniture. The grandfather clock which had ticked away so innocently for years suddenly appeared to be a long, lean figure which peered furtively at him with narrow eyes.

And why was the clock ticking so loudly? Tick tock, tick tock, tick tock… he imagined for a moment that someone had turned the volume up, but even Nathan knew that there are no volume controls on an 18th century long-case clock.

The clock struck midnight; the silent pause that followed suggested that someone was waiting. Suddenly Nathan just wanted to get out, out of this stuffy, spooky, weird place and back on the street where he belonged.

In his heavy stupor he tripped over the arm of the rocking chair which he had pushed into the corner and careered headlong into the wall. The wall shook, and his grandmother's beloved encyclopaedia, on the high shelf above him, toppled, swayed and fell.

Nathan did not even see its silent descent. The encyclopaedia's sharp corner, heavily armoured with gilded metal, smashed through the top of his skull as decisively as a builder's hammer through a panel of plasterboard.

The final lesson had been delivered. And beside Nathan's inert and bleeding body, the rocking chair in the corner of the room began to rock gently back and forth.

TEATIME FOR TEDDY BEARS

Kathleen had been mad about teddy bears ever since she had been a little girl, several decades before. Every aspect of her life revolved around them. She was so besotted with them that she frequently began to believe that she was a teddy bear herself. She even had a name for herself for use whenever she became a teddy – 'Snouty.'

She had two large teddy bears which were particularly important to her, and having lived alone with them for many years, she had long since come to regard them as her brother and sister. Her real brother and sister had both died rather suddenly as youngsters; Kathleen had never been told just how it had happened. The two bears had belonged to her grandmother before her, so in bear years they were now almost prehistoric.

The bigger of the two was dressed in blue, so of course he was called Bluey. The other was in pink, so you can imagine what he, or rather she, was called. Kathleen took Bluey and Pinky everywhere. She even took them for rides in her shopping trolley. Sometimes they took turns in 'driving' the car, and they would go to the hairdresser's in a carrier bag so they could get a 'Teddy Bear' cut.

Her obsession got her into serious trouble on one occasion when she was stopped on suspicion of drinking and driving and tried to convince the arresting officer, only half joking, that Pinky was driving the car. The officer only let her go with a caution because he could not think of anything to charge her with.

Bluey and Pinky were not the best-looking bears in the world. Their fur was badly faded and stained, the felt on their paws was worn and even their faces didn't look quite right; Bluey had an odd cross-eyed grin, while Pinky's over-large and staring eyes gave her a peculiarly obsessive look, as if she had been staying awake with the aid of stimulants for rather too long. Unusually for teddies of their vintage, both bears had long, fully-jointed arms which bent in towards their tummies. Bluey was always dressed in a waistcoat and spotted bow tie, which made him look quite self-confident, whilst Pinky wore an old woollen shawl and a badly-torn straw hat through which one of her tattered ears stuck straight up in the air and the other flopped right over. Yet despite all their cumulative age-related deficiencies, Kathleen continued to be besotted with them.

They were warm and cuddly, always there to listen sympathetically to her moans and woes, always offering a furry shoulder to cry on. They never interrupted her, nor told her to snap out of it if she was depressed, and were always around when she needed them.

Depending on the quality of the light and the position she put them in, she was able to get them to look quite different and with their expressive, lived-in faces she could persuade them to convey distinctive moods.

Kathleen's favourite summer pastime was to take the bears on a lovely picnic in a glade at the bottom of her very large garden. So it was that she told them one glorious late afternoon in June to be good bears whilst she prepared for a special picnic to celebrate her birthday. She carried a freshly-ironed tablecloth over one arm and a tray on which were placed a jug of orange squash, a jug of milk for the bears, mugs decorated with teddy bear characters and two plates carrying banana and egg sandwiches which were no bigger than postage stamps, along with biscuits and coffee cake. She crossed the upper and lower lawns, where the hydrangeas, laburnum and yellow azaleas were all in bloom, then walked past a rockery full of dianthus, phlox and gentian, before finally making her way into the glade and laying the tablecloth on a large tartan rug. She then placed large bunches of buttercups around the seating area, where she lovingly placed her faithful teddies.

Following a relaxing couple of hours enjoying the picnic, 'Snouty', Bluey and Pinky then proceeded to sing songs, tell each other stories and play some games, after which Kathleen dozed off in the late afternoon sunshine, a warm smile on her face.

Bluey stirred, stretched and turned to Pinky.

'I'm a bad bear, I am,' muttered Bluey, nodding his head and winking at his companion. 'And SHE hasn't given me enough to eat, as usual. I'm still hungry.'

'So am I' replied Pinky. 'Cakes and sandwiches are all very well, but they're not what bears like best, are they?'

The two bears grinned at each other.

The sun slipped behind a cloud. Teddy bears can't hold things, since they don't have fingers, just useless half-moons of felt at the ends of their arms, but they can hold a knife all right when it's pressed between two paws, and their fully-jointed arms can exert a surprising amount of downward pressure.

Sometimes, something very nasty gets packed inside teddies along with their straw stuffing. Bluey and Pink had waited a long time for this moment. Now 'Snouty' was about to be savoured in the same way as her long-deceased siblings had been so many years before.

'If you go down to the woods today, you'd better not go alone
It's a lovely day in the woods today, but safer to stay at home…'

THE WIND FARM

Stephen wondered whether perhaps he suffered from anemomenophobia. He had come across the term the previous day, and learned that it was the fear of wind turbines, and he rather liked it – the word, not the fear. He had learned that those big, white rotating blades apparently scared the living daylights out of some people, who thought of them as evil, possessed, a bad omen. Some anemomenophobics even associated wind-turbines with huge, alien life-forms, which would make a pretty good theme for a disaster movie, he reflected.

He also learned that compared to the surrounding areas, the climate in the immediate vicinity of a wind farm is cooler during the day and slightly warmer during the night.

The reason why Stephen had wondered whether he suffered from this particular phobia was that the first time he had seen a wind turbine, he had found himself unable to breathe. He had no idea why. Yet despite an odd kind of terror, he had also felt a weird fascination, even an admiration for them. He thought some of them looked quite beautiful. Goodness knows what a psychiatrist would make of that.

There was a wind farm high on a hillside close to the northern village where he lived. Each time he passed it on his journey to work he would gaze up at the turbines on their distant hillside and wonder what it would be like to stand right under one of them. Winter twilight was the best time to appreciate them, because then they took on a bewitching white tone against the grey of the darkening sky, particularly if the land was covered in snow. There they stood through the seasons, their snow-white blades whirling in space like distant angels beckoning unseen guests.

Stephen's wind farm was relatively small, with just nine turbines, although when the light from the setting sun fell on them at a particular angle, he could have sworn there were ten of them. On closer inspection the next morning he was always reassured that there were indeed just nine.

Having viewed them from a distance twice a day for almost a year on his commute to and from work, Stephen had a sudden impulse to experience what they were like up close. And to be fair to them, they did appear to be offering him a friendly invitation into the fields where they worked and rested.

So it was that on a late November day he set forth to make acquaintance with the giant, mystical figures on the hill. He buttoned up his coat against the rising wind and trudged up the lonely roadway which, he had calculated, would take him ultimately to the high ground where they stood.

With a strange sensation of excitement, tempered with a certain trepidation, he reached the upper slopes of the mountain. Here the ordered structure of fieldwork gave way to areas of rough scrubland and ultimately to the high expanse of peat bog which formed the setting for the wind turbines, set deeply within formidable man-made foundations of rock and concrete.

As he arrived amongst them he found himself surrounded by the whooshing, buzzing sound emanating from the turbines, rising and falling on the wind. The sound had a curiously vocal quality, as if they were speaking to him. He was suddenly aware just how far away he now was from the rest of humanity. Around him was nothing but the uncompromising vastness of the wide hill country all around, and beyond that, nothing but the grey November sky.

The long shadows of the turbines were now racing across the darkening bog and becoming blacker by the second as the sun sank towards the horizon. With the night pulling down its nocuous shades, Stephen suddenly felt an urgent desire to get away from the place, to regain the safety of civilisation. Suddenly it seemed to him that each of the great turbines was looming over him with a yearning malevolence, as if they were searching for something they wanted, and in him they hoped to find it. He felt their hunger, their eagerness, their expectation. He began to wonder why on earth he had wanted to come to this godforsaken place.

It was time to go. He started to walk back the way he had come, but within a yard or two he found the coarse grass at his feet giving way to springy soil, then mud. Perhaps it was time to turn back and find another way, but as even as the thought came to him, he found his feet sinking into putrescent black liquid. In alarm he tried to pull his left foot up, only to find the increased weight on the right foot immediately drove his leg up to the knee.

Stephen realised with mounting terror that he was truly stuck, and sinking almost as fast as if he were going down in a lift. He gazed around in desperation, but there was not so much as a blade of grass within reach for him to seize on to. He tried to throw himself forward, but the mud quickly welcomed his torso as eagerly as it had his feet and legs. A black horizon rose remorselessly around him, and he gasped in panic as he felt the pressure reach his chest. He tried to scream, but it was far too late for that. The noise was stifled by the pressure on his rib cage.

Now he was up to his shoulders, and he could feel the last of his energy draining away. He waved his arms in desperation at the rapidly-setting sun, while above him the turbines waved back, humming and swooshing impassively. Within a few minutes, they would once again be the only visible signs of man's presence in this remote spot. It was far too late for Stephen to worry about whether or not he suffered from anemomenophobia.

BIRDS HAVE LONG MEMORIES

Uncle Jacob disliked most birds, but he detested crows and rooks with a vengeance. He had been born and bred at Northwood Farm, which had been in his family for generations and which, on the death of his father, he had inherited, farming it all on his own. I was his only remaining relative and I did my best to help him out whenever I could, which was almost every weekend.

My uncle's abhorrence of crows and his determination to kill as many of them as he could became an overwhelming obsession. It lasted all year round, but it reached its peak during the planting season. His cornfields were sometimes completely destroyed by the rooks, without a single ear left intact. Every year during their flocking phase in the early winter months, thousands of noisy birds overwhelmed the farm's surrounding trees and buildings, causing structural damage, harassing his herd of milking cows and posing a serious risk to his health from their foul droppings. Their madly-flapping wings and piercing, torturous cries drove him to despair. He tried everything possible to destroy as many of them as he could, spending an hour or so every day shooting them. In one field he placed a crude scarecrow made from weathered wood and a hollowed pumpkin which he adorned with his old clothes. In another he hung an effigy of a dead crow upside down. He set bird netting, traps and spikes, but to little avail. The problem was that the birds were highly intelligent, and they quickly changed their behaviour to avoid everything my uncle attempted in order to get rid of them. The huge flock appeared to be in constant, raucous communication with each other, sounding like fingernails on a chalkboard. They shuffled around, their beady eyes protruding from their darting heads, searching for any opportunity to cause mischief.

Every morning just after dawn all the rooks left the roost for part of the day; all except for one. The biggest bird always remained. It stationed itself at the top of the tallest tree beside the farmhouse, never making a sound, and followed my uncle when he set out, shadowing him wherever he went, always just beyond the range of a shotgun.

So it was that under a melancholy sky on a grey Sunday morning, as the first breaths of winter caused the large trees around the farmhouse to groan their discomfort against the cold, I made a grisly discovery amongst the rustling stalks of winter barley. There in the dirt was a huge mass of dead rooks, some of their jet-black feathers reddened with congealed blood, whilst others fluttered gently in the chilly wind. There were hundreds of them.

With a mixture of revulsion and anguish I went out, to find more dead birds littering the farmyard and to my horror several others inside each and every room of the farmhouse. What could possibly have been responsible for such carnage?

I sought the answer from my uncle, but he was nowhere to be seen. The only living presence was the great, solitary rook, which stood still perched on the farmhouse roof. It looked directly at me.

I was disturbed by the utter quietness that had fallen over the house. No doubt my uncle would provide me with some answers, but I became increasingly anxious as night fell without his appearance.

I decided to sleep overnight at the farm to await his homecoming, but following a restless night I was awoken in the morning by a soft knocking at the bedroom window. I drew back the curtains and was confronted by the beady eyes of the black sentinel, the great rook which always harassed my uncle. Beyond it I saw thousands more of its kind, all apparently embarked on an orgy of destruction. It seemed they were attacking everything that belonged to my uncle. I could even hear them on top of the farmhouse tearing off the roof tiles.

I ran outside to scare them off, but I immediately knew I was wasting my time. The damage they had inflicted on the farm and on all its assets, buildings and crops was almost complete. The prime herd of cattle had not only been slaughtered by a thousand vicious stabs of the rooks' bills, the carcasses had been stripped to their bones.

Bewildered and in a state of profound shock, I wandered aimlessly around the farm. I could barely comprehend the total destruction that had been ministered.

Then at the back of one field I saw a large flock of the birds clustered around something; obviously the scarecrow. It too had fallen foul of the murderous, black-feathered aggressors. Its shredded clothes fluttered in the wind, the head tilting crazily to one side, the skeletal jaw hanging loosely. Its eyes were just empty holes.

As I drew closer, the shifting mass of black wings parted, and the birds hurtled away screaming into the sky. I looked down at the mayhem they had left behind.

It was not the scarecrow. It was Uncle Jacob, and the carrion fowl had stripped his corpse to the bones.

ONCE UPON A TIME

Long, long ago, a young delinquent was guilty of such wilfully malign behaviour that she was institutionalised for her own protection and for the well-being of everyone else. This youngster's notoriety was such that it became the substance of several stories which have been laid down in history but, believe me, almost all these stories have become distorted with the passage of time.

Our young friend had been a very busy little delinquent indeed. One story would have us believe that Cinderella's step-sisters cut off parts of their own feet in order to fit them into a glass slipper in the hope that they would fool a prince. The prince was apparently alerted to this con by two pigeons which pecked out the step-sisters' eyes, and they had to spend the rest of their lives as blind, lame beggars while Cinderella lived in luxury with the Prince.

Are we really expected to believe that anyone would do that to their own feet? It was our young reprobate who consorted with Cinders in undertaking this vile act. Then there was all that misinformation about poor little Snow White. It wasn't her wicked step-mother who wanted her dead, it was her mother. And she didn't just want Snow White's heart – she wanted her liver and lungs as well, so she hired someone dressed as a servant to take Snow White into the woods. When the queen showed up at Snow White's wedding, someone dressed as a servant forced her to step into iron shoes that had been cooking in a fire, and then forced her to dance until she died. Our perverted young friend liked to dress up.

I'm sure you remember the occasion when Jack went up the hill with Jill and he subsequently broke his crown. Well, what that actually means is that poor Jack was beheaded. Have you ever wondered who it was that caused Jack's gruesome demise?

Jill didn't fare much better either. Some sort of 'witch' apparently cut off Rapunzel's hair and used it to lure a good-looking young man into a high tower, then hurled him off the top of it, letting him fall into a thorn bush that plucked out his eyes. Charming! This was the same cannibalistic 'witch' that lured Hansel and Gretel into her cottage in an attempt to roast them alive before eating them. Mind you, she wanted to bleed the children on a sawhorse first.

Not only did our psychopathic young friend like to dress up, she had a particular penchant for dressing up as a witch. Whilst we're on the subject of psychopaths, the word 'contrary' used to be one way of describing a murderous psychopath. It doesn't therefore say much for Mary, who really was quite 'contrary' and wasn't a keen gardener at all but was in fact a young homicidal maniac whose silver bells and cockleshells were torture devices, not garden accoutrements. No wonder she was institutionalised at a young age – this was shortly after she killed Cock Robin, then collected his blood and had his grave dug. When she was undergoing therapy inside a House of Correction she nonchalantly admitted to cutting off the tails of some members of Bo Peep's woolpack and hanging them on a tree to dry in a secluded meadow. She also confessed to pretending to be a queen and that she deliberately made an old imp called Rumpelstiltskin so annoyed that he drove his right foot so far into the ground that it sank all the way up to his waist; then in a raving passion he seized his left foot with both hands and tore himself in two.

During a violent temper tantrum of her own which she experienced just after her release from the House of Correction, it didn't take her long to hurl the Frog Prince against a wall, after which she cut off his head.

You know when the three blind mice ran after the farmer's wife and she cut off their tails with a carving knife? Don't believe a word of it – the farmer's wife is just an allusion. This enthusiasm for torture and death was entirely that possessed by our youthful degenerate. I'll leave you to work out how she blinded the mice – it's no wonder they ran!

What sort of a young mind leads a person to perform such acts of depravity? What sort of a person has the criminal mentality that drives them to be so cruel to others without showing any remorse whatsoever? It's the kind of person who always wears a hoodie and a cape the colour of blood and goes deep into a dark forest to discuss with a wolf how best to 'take care' of her very own grandmother.

THROUGH THE EYES OF OTHERS

It was a Sunday afternoon in late November when John Garrett slowly approached the village in his old banger of a car. It was barely four o'clock, but because of some low-lying mist it was already beginning to get dark.

Fed up with the stresses and strains of daily life, John had decided it was time to take a short break, and being a lover of solitude and having no family ties, he had made up his mind to drive into the countryside for a few days. When he had set out that morning, he had decided to go wherever the road took him, since he was determined to enjoy as many adventures as his destiny directed. With just one stop for something to eat, he had driven all day, initially through pleasant countryside dotted with quaint villages, meandering rivers and picturesque towns boasting buildings with striking architectural features. But as the day had progressed, his route had become more mundane and isolated. Flat, featureless farmland stretched endlessly for several miles in every direction, telephone and power lines providing the only signs of life, all the way to the distant horizon. And to make matters worse, a fog was coming down.

The solitary village at which he had now arrived was surrounded by fallow, empty fields. He was struck by the complete stillness that greeted him when he stopped at what appeared to be the centre of the village. There was just enough misty light for him to see that the village had no church, but there was a monument erected from a few large, dusty stones and there were two cemeteries, one on each side of the road, which gave him the uneasy feeling that the dead lay all around him.

By the roadside he noticed a number of gaunt and emaciated dog carcasses which he assumed were the consequences of starvation. He could see the ramshackle structures of a few houses, but he saw no bustling people, no barking dogs and no other signs of life. From the houses came none of the expected sounds of laughter and conversation, only a deathly silence; and he noted with a chill that despite the cold and the thickening fog, not a single chimney had smoke coming out of it. It seemed to him that any semblance of humanity and hope had long gone, as if life itself had nothing left to give.

And then he saw a figure crossing the road in front of

him and braked to a stop. Now, at last, he could see people; but what strange people! As he peered out of the car window into the gloom, he made out the shapes of several bent human figures with dark faces fumbling their way through the murk. They looked like departed spirits looking for something, as if searching for long-lost homes and loved ones. He watched as, confused and disorientated, they groped and stumbled their way along the pavement, while the mist swirled between the houses and bare trees.

Suddenly, to his alarm, the figure of a man appeared, looming above the windscreen. John's hand darted to the door lock, but he was too late to prevent the man wrenching open the door and thrusting his face inside the car. The eyes were hollow and hooded, and as his face caught the dim light for a moment John, frozen with horror, saw that the man's eye sockets were empty. A bony hand came out and touched John's face. It felt like the wings of moths brushing his skin.

To his relief the man slowly withdrew his head and in seeking some protection, John locked the doors from within; or at least he did his best, for the locks on the old car were worn and unreliable. And then, looking around him, he realised that all these people were the same. None of them had eyes. Just like the dead, they stared blindly into infinity.

The figures shambled away one by one until John and his car were alone again. The fog was now so dense that driving further was all but impossible. Having made sure that his doors were secure, he pulled his car rug over him and spent a cold, restless and largely sleepless night in his car.

The mist had disappeared by the time he awoke the next morning and there was no sign of any of the mysterious people. Anxious to stretch his legs and relieve himself, he got out of the car and locked it carefully behind him. It was then that he noticed the figure of an old woman who was kneeling in front of a stone monument in the centre of the village's main street. She seemed to be picking bulbs out of an old metal bucket and planting them in the soil in front of the monument.

John went up to her, curious to discover what she was about, and asked if he could offer any assistance.

'Leave me!' she cried. 'My sins will find me, I shall be punished! Only through the eyes of others can we see our own faults. I have sinned all my life and I must atone before it's too late – only through the eyes of others – through the eyes of others.'

Clearly the woman was unhinged. There was nothing he could do for her but leave her to continue her harmless ramblings. But then he looked down at the contents of the bucket.

The round objects in the woman's bucket were not bulbs. They were eyes – human eyes. He recoiled in shock.

'Where did these come from? What are you doing?' he asked her in alarm.

'It matters little to me if they can no longer distinguish between day and night,' she replied. 'I have taken what I need. I must atone. Through the eyes of others, I must atone.'

The unearthly horror of the woman's expression filled John with fear. He backed away, then raced back to his car, unlocked it, jumped in and drove off at some speed.

He was some distance outside the village before he noticed something in the mirror – his coat? The car rug? But it was moving…

He screeched to a halt and turned round. This was not possible! It was the old woman. Somehow she had got into the back seat of the car.

'How did you… what are you doing?' said John. The woman's eyes were full of tears. Her body went rigid as she struggled to hold them back.

Then she appeared to make up her mind. She raised the knife in her right hand, and her expression of misery and grief slowly changed to a cunning grin. She extended her bony left hand and gripped John around the neck with an impossibly powerful grip.

'You have such nice green eyes,' she said.

THE CROSSING

Throughout his long life Tommy Christmas had considered himself to be a very lucky man. He had a loving and supportive wife, three wonderful daughters and two beautiful grandchildren. He adored them all, and they adored Big Tommy Christmas right back. He'd also been fortunate enough to have spent almost all his working life running a care home for disadvantaged kids, a role which he had enjoyed immensely and from which he had derived a great deal of satisfaction.

On his retirement, Tommy felt equally fortunate in landing a job as a lollipop man at the very school which his grandchildren attended. He was immensely proud of being one of the longest serving members of the School Crossing Patrol Service, having seen children safely across the road for almost a decade. He treated all the kids as though they were his own, greeting them with high fives when he saw them on each schoolday morning and again in the afternoon, or pretending to be a soldier standing to attention in the middle of the road, or giving impressions of popular children's TV characters. Because of his name and his considerable kindness, the youngsters, and indeed their parents, referred to him as Father Christmas, which he considered a great compliment.

Tommy discharged his responsibilities with the utmost dedication, teaching each child to follow his instructions and not to step into the road until he signalled to them that it was safe to do so. He always looked forward to donning his high-visibility fluorescent coat and hat, and was invariably at his post at least half an hour before and after he needed to be. Like most of his kind around the country, most of his days went without a hitch except for the occasional mishap, which was almost always the fault of a careless or inattentive driver, but almost all of them had the good grace to signal an apology when they realised their errors.

Everything changed one late October afternoon. When Tommy stepped out into the highway in order to stop the traffic so that the schoolchildren could cross the road, a young idiot in a high-performance car decided to drive directly at Tommy, accelerating as he did so and only swerving aside at the last moment. Tommy managed to avoid injury by the skin of his teeth, but he was badly shaken by the experience, not to say furious.

And then the very next week, it happened again. This time the driver's behaviour was even more reckless. He steered his car at a group of three children who had already started to cross the road under Tommy's guidance. Fortunately Tommy saw the car in time to scoop them out of the way, but it was a close-run thing.

This time Tommy managed to get the registration number of the offender's car and reported the matter to the police. However they showed little interest, as there had been no collision and no injuries, and in any case, it would be one person's word against another's.

And that wasn't the last time. The appalling antics of the maniacal young driver continued. He would wait until Tommy was off guard and pull off the same stunt again, never injuring anyone, but always leaving behind a furious lollipop man and a group of terrified children.

Tommy's frustration at the failure of the police to do anything about the maniac led him to make some enquiries about the ownership of the car. He finally tracked down the young idiot, whose name was Shane, to a house on a council estate, and knocked on his door late one evening to give him a piece of his mind. The young thug couldn't have cared less. He simply laughed in Tommy's face, telling him he would drive his car as fast as he liked and advising him with relish exactly where he could stick his ★★★★★★ lollipop.

All this was not the best medicine for a man of Tommy's age who had never coped well with stress. He started to lose sleep, and became increasingly anxious and depressed. His powerful frame was becoming lean and gaunt, and it was clear his health was not going to allow him to take on the responsibility of a crossing warden for very much longer.

Then it happened. One morning Shane failed to hit the brakes in time, and his car struck a young mother as she was crossing the road under Tommy's direction. She was hospitalised for months, and was told she would never walk again. This time there was a prosecution and a trial, but of course Shane denied the charge and lied in the faces of the judge and the prosecuting counsel. In the end, because someone at police HQ had failed to follow the correct procedures for handling evidence, the case was dismissed on a technicality.

The council handled Tommy's departure diplomatically; they sent him a letter recognising his excellent service and gave him a grateful send-off. But for Tommy it was the ultimate insult, to be sacked because of the evil, malicious doings of someone who did not deserve to breathe the same air as the children in his charge.

Tommy's last day was the day before the Christmas holidays. Once the children had all been seen safely off on their way home, he would have to hand in his precious lollipop for ever. He had just a few days to work out his plan.

Fortunately, when the day came, Shane did not disappoint Tommy. He heard the roar of the approaching sports car bang on time, just as he had finished shepherding the second lot of children across the road, all dressed up in their Christmas party costumes. Tommy just had time to see Shane's look of puzzlement, then growing horror, as instead of jumping out of the way of the car, Tommy grinned defiantly at Shane, raised his lollipop, swung it around so that the bottom end was towards the windscreen, and hurled it with all his strength. The big round disc at the rear end kept the pole straight and true in flight. The leading end, expertly fitted in Tommy's workshop at home with a steel point from a school javelin 'borrowed' from the sports field stores shed, punched through the glass and struck Shane squarely in his gawping open mouth. Such was the combined speed of pole and car that the point passed straight through Shane's head and skewered his twitching form to the seat. Tommy's aim could not have been better.

When they pulled what was left of the old lollipop man from under the car, he still bore a look of triumph on his battered features.

DEAD TIME

The distinctive saddleback tower of the ancient church had long been used as a landmark by the inhabitants of the village and by travellers making their way to more distant destinations. The church tower, which had a history stretching back to the 7th Century, housed a large bell which bore the Latin inscription *te enim campana* – the bell tolls for thee. Because of its age, the bell could be rung only by striking it with a hammer.

Alice leaned on the left pillar of the churchyard gate so that she could regain her breath after climbing the steep pathway leading up from the lane below. On top of the pillar was a horizontal sundial, the shadow cast by its long thin rod pointing directly between her eyes.

She had taken up genealogy soon after her retirement and was keen to explore the graveyard for useful information about her ancestors, who were buried in the family grave. She had been born and bred in the village and still regularly attended the church, but she had always felt uneasy when visiting both the church and its graveyard. The smell of old earth filled the air, mould-covered gravestones peppered the graveyard and weeds covered those graves which loved ones had long stopped visiting because, by now, they too had joined their relatives under the soil.

Rows of tombstones stood erect and silent, most of them cracked and crumbling with the weathering of the centuries and some leaning over as though listening to the dead who lay directly under them. It seemed as though the graveyard was full of rotting boxes containing decaying bodies and unfulfilled dreams; the weak and the powerful, the rich and the poor, all now united and equal in death.

All graves hold secrets; it was just as well Alice didn't know that some of those within the graveyard were in fact completely empty. She knew she had to hurry to find what she was looking for, since the night was quickly closing in. She had visited the family grave before, so she knew where it was and what she was looking for.

She examined the gravestone and recorded all the information she needed from the engravings on it. She was about to leave for home when she noticed a freshly-engraved entry under her late mother's name. It read: 'In loving memory of Alice Fielding. Born 2nd January 1941/Died 12th March 2008.'

Alice fell backwards in shock. But *she* was **Alice Fielding** - and January 2 1941 was her date of birth!

There was no one else in the family with the same name, and certainly none who had been born on the same day. What on earth was going on?

Her first thought was that someone had made a mistake and put the wrong details of a recent burial on the stone, though she could not imagine how such a thing could happen. Alice could not help feeling extremely uneasy. She was at a loss to think what could have led someone to make such a ridiculous error. She decided she would take the matter up with the vicar first thing in the morning. There had to be some innocent explanation; she just couldn't imagine what it was.

On her way back towards the churchyard gates, she heard the church bell start to toll. This too was odd, as she knew no one had entered the church. And then she heard, very faintly, the voices of children playing somewhere in the distance. She listened, trying to work out where they were coming from. She heard one of the voices call her own name – 'Lissy! Lissy!' This was becoming more and more peculiar. And who would call her Lissy? She hadn't been called that since she had been a child.

She walked to the corner by the church and looked around, but now the voices seemed to be coming from behind her.

She was now standing by the family grave again. As she turned to look at it once more, she had another shock. Her mother was standing by it, looking as large as life. She was smiling gently at Alice. Behind her – yes, there was her father too, apparently digging up the grave. A lighted candle shone at the base of the headstone.

Alice let out a gasp of fear and turned to run out of the churchyard. As she did so, the church clock began to strike. Standing in the lane behind the gates was a hearse; an old-fashioned one drawn by four black horses. Someone was calling her name – 'Alice, Alice!' and now a hand had seized her shoulder…

Gradually Alice realised that she was emerging from a deep sleep. The voice was her husband Tony's, and the hand on her shoulder was his warm, familiar hand trying to wake her from her ordeal.

'You've been having a nightmare, love' he said. 'Everything's OK. Now you just lie here and get your breath back while I go and make us a nice cup of tea.'

Thank god! The feeling of relief that washed over her when she realised it all been just a terrible dream was immeasurable. Except – if only that awful pain in her chest would go away. What on earth was it? She tried to call down to her husband to bring up some of her tablets, but she did not seem to be able to get the words out.

She lay still for a moment, and to her relief the pain

ebbed away and she was suffused with a warm, relaxed feeling. But then she noticed something very odd. Even though the mirror on the wall was directly opposite her, try as she might she couldn't see herself in it as usual. There was the bed and the rumpled stack of pillows she was lying on, but of herself there was no sign. Very strange. Whatever was going on?

She turned to look at the digital clock-calendar beside her bed. She had always liked that clock, ever since she had bought it on a Christmas shopping trip to New York some years previously. It advised her that the time was 06:03 and today was 03-12-08.

But now the image of the clock was dissolving and fading, and the whole room seemed to be slipping into nothingness...

It had not occurred to Alice in her last seconds on this earth that because the month and the day on the clock were the opposite way round compared to English clocks, it was showing the date she had seen on the mysterious headstone entry: March 12th 2008.

A LIFE LESS ORDINARY

Everyone who knew Hannah Tibbit agreed that she was an extremely boring person. The only thing that was remotely interesting about her was that both her forename and surname read the same backwards as they did forwards. The problem was that she felt the need to bring this fact to everybody's attention, regardless of the number of times she had already told them. Beyond that Hannah had virtually nothing else to impart to the few people she could count as friends, who, in the main, were her long-suffering colleagues in the library where she had worked all her life. She had no friends, no partner and her neighbours avoided her with a vengeance. She showed little enthusiasm for anything at all. She had no imagination, no ambition, no hobbies, no opinions, no plans, no interests, no sense of humour and very little personality. She usually talked about depressing matters such as the rising crime rate and the falling value of her savings. She did not even enliven her conversation by saying bad things about other people. Understandably, she rarely smiled, and she never laughed.

At home, Hannah's routine and diet never changed. She always stayed at home during her annual leave, always watched the same television programmes and always patronised the same shops. Her principal subject of conversation was the most boring one of all; herself. In short, she was a thoroughly tedious person.

At work, in contrast to her colleagues, Hannah never tried to be innovative or creative about the way she presented books and literature to the members of the library. She simply continued to do her job in exactly the same way she had always done it, week in, week out. This was a great shame, since the children in particular were keen to learn and sought inspiration from wherever they could find it.

Everyone knew that Hannah was terminally boring – except, of course, Hannah herself. She had no idea just how dull her personality was, and this made her become even more dreadfully tedious as she grew older.

At last, the disengaging effect she had on her colleagues and her profoundly negative approach to her role in the library prompted her manager to confront her directly, in an effort to inspire her to become more engaging and less terminally tedious. But Hannah couldn't understand what the problem was; she didn't think she was at all boring. To prove it to her manager and her colleagues, Hannah did perhaps the first even faintly interesting thing she had ever done in her life. She came up with a plan which was intended to show them that she could be as inventive as anyone else. Thinking outside the box was an extremely rare event where Hannah was concerned, but to her credit, her plan sounded quite intriguing to her colleagues, who nevertheless all remained sceptical about whether she would actually be able to go through with it.

Hannah's plan was to choose one book at random from each section of the library, open it, again at random, and perform, construct or enact whatever was described or detailed on the selected page. She started with the gardening section; the task described on the page involved the planting of a dwarf conifer. Really quite interesting. Next was cookery, which required her to prepare a simple sponge cake. Hardly challenging, but as the baking of cakes was among the many life skills she had failed to acquire, she ended up with a cake the shape and consistency of a dartboard.

For photography, she opened a page of a how-to-do-it guide which instructed her to take a self-portrait with an interesting background. As a backdrop, she chose the dwarf conifer she had just planted. Then for indoor games and pastimes, she played herself, for several hours, at the thrilling game of Patience.

Undertaking a sea crossing was the task demanded of her in the page from the book she selected from the foreign travel section. This was more of a challenge, but she managed to cut it down to size by taking a day return trip on the Isle of Wight Ferry. The book she plucked from the shelves on local interest and history required her to gather information from a reliable source, so she chose to make a visit to the very library where she worked, on her day off. Because she went there by bus, this also covered the needs of the transport section, which required her 'to experience the adventure of public transport'.

Drawing a still-life image was the task required in the arts and crafts section, so she drew, very badly, her own newly-planted conifer. For British Travel she did not perform a new challenge, as she felt her voyage to the Isle of Wight allowed her to tick that box, and she had had quite enough adventure for one year.

And so it went on – she complied with all the challenges in the most tedious and unimaginative ways possible.

The very last section she picked was the one entitled 'Horror and the Macabre'. Many of the books here were large, old and faded, and it was not at all obvious what most of them were about, until you took them down from the shelf and examined them.

She decided to pick a thick and very dusty book on

one of the higher shelves, drew it carefully down and opened it. The paper was old, coarse and yellowing and the type archaic and smudged. The page she had opened bore the title 'Dancing with Demons'.

Hannah had managed to take up all her previous challenges, but this was a very different matter. She was not going to have anything to do with dancing, and certainly not with demons. The very idea!

'Utter rubbish!' snorted Hannah loudly. 'There are most certainly no such things as demons, devils, ghosts or any other such claptrap!' She slammed the book shut with a sniff and lifted it back towards the shelf. But to her horror, as the book drew level with the shelf, a hand emerged from the gap where the book had been sitting; a long, skeletal right hand. The long, bony fingers seized her podgy wrist and held her fast. As Hannah began to scream in terror, an equally long and bony left hand emerged from the same aperture and seized her by her throat, instantly stifling her cries. The two hands now joined fingers around Hannah's neck, and began to squeeze.

Hannah's terrified gurgle gave way to a muffled gasp, then a desperate choking as the bony fingers tightened on her windpipe. There was a moment's silence, then Hannah's feet kicked a couple of times and she hung still. The disembodied hand unlocked itself from her throat and

Hannah's lifeless body slumped to the floor, raising a small cloud of dust motes which danced in the light.

For the first and last time in her life, Hannah Tibbit had done something truly interesting.

THE SILENCE OF THE BIRDS

Dai 'Gold Top' Morgan had worked for the Greenfields Dairy for almost three decades. His customers, friends and colleagues all called him 'Gold Top' because he had straw-coloured hair, and because the bottles of full-fat milk he delivered to the customers of Greenfields Dairy came with a gold-coloured foil top.

Dai loved his job as a milkman, but it had one very significant drawback – he had to be at work by 5.30 on each workday morning. This unhappy state of affairs was compounded by the fact that Dai suffered from insomnia, which became more severe as he grew older. The harder he tried to get to sleep, the longer he would take to drift off, because he would lie in his bed constantly worrying about the adverse effect of sleep deprivation on his health.

The spring and summer months were the worst, because he always slept with the window wide open, and while Dai woke early every morning, the birds woke even earlier. They had become the bane of his life. It wasn't that he didn't like birds - he regularly placed scraps of mouldy cheese or curd snack left over from the dairy on the bird-table in his garden – but he soon became desperate to put a stop to the ceaseless early morning avian racket which prevented him from getting adequate rest.

His next-door neighbour Ted worked for the Environmental Department at the local council, so one night on the way home from the pub, Dai asked him for advice on how to get rid of the noisy pests.

'It's not the noise of the birds that keeps *me* awake in the mornings,' grumbled his neighbour. 'I'm surprised you can hear them over the noise of your milk bottles.'

The following morning was the worst Dai had ever experienced. The din emanating from the gulls over the nearby estuary was deafening – they were making constant high-pitched squawks and squeals, almost as though they were laughing at him. They were still at it when he left the house at 5 am.

'I'd give anything to get rid of those pesky seagulls,' he muttered as he got into his car.

It soon seemed as though his wish was being granted, because Dai found that over the course of the following week, the cries of the seagulls gradually subsided until they eventually stopped altogether. However, a new problem then arose with the equally noisy, unmusical, staccato screeches of a pair of magpies, which now began to wake him at the crack of dawn every day. He cursed them loudly one morning when he left for work and wished he could be rid of them. To his amazement the cries of the magpies also gradually disappeared after that, just as those of the seagulls had.

In due course the hollow cooing of the pigeons, the clanging, jarring, raucous calls of the crows and the hoarse cackling of the jackdaws all went the same way as the racket which had been inflicted on poor Dai by the seagulls and magpies. Within the course of a couple of weeks they all fell silent. Dai couldn't believe his good fortune; he hadn't slept so well for many a year.

And so it continued, until the early hours of a late September night. In the hour of silence just before dawn when nothing breathes and everything seems transfixed, Dai awoke suddenly from his slumber to see a large, shadowy object perched on the footboard at the bottom of his bed. There before him was the owner of the night, the stalker of the dusk and the dawn, its deep orange-red, saucer-like eyes stared relentlessly at him. It was a gigantic European eagle owl, nearly three feet high, with demonic horned tufts of feathers on its head, a bird which eats buzzards for breakfast and foxes for supper. Dai knew none of this of course; he just knew that he was looking at an owl the size of a refrigerator.

Dai sat bolt upright in shock. And then he thought he must surely be dreaming, because the damn thing spoke to him.

'Good morning Mr Morgan, did you sleep well?' asked the owl, its head moving rapidly sideways and back and forth. 'You should have had a very peaceful night. I've done everything you asked of me. You may have noticed that I've taken care of all those tiresome birds. It was the least I could do for you, since you were kind enough to leave me all that food on your garden table.'

'What do you want?' Dai managed to stammer in shock, clutching the bedclothes with trembling fingers. Surely he had not been taking any drugs that could have caused a hallucination as convincing and terrifying as this one?

'The roadkill your neighbour leaves me is much nicer than the dairy scraps I get from you' answered the owl, 'and he's really fed up with the appalling racket you make with your milk bottles every morning.'

The owl released one massive, scaly talon from the footboard and revolved its head. Its huge hooked beak caught the light of the window as it turned. It slowly closed and then reopened one eye. It seemed almost to be winking at him.

'So' said the owl. 'One good turn deserves another, don't you think?'

The owl lifted its bulk soundlessly into the air, stretching its wings almost the width of the bed, and launched itself gracefully and silently at its prey.

FOR MY LAST TRICK...

Despite old Harold Lamb's eccentric and doddery nature – or maybe because of it – he was well liked by the inhabitants of the village in which he lived. A gentle soul, he had always appeared absent-minded, rather clumsy and a little introverted. He lived in a ramshackle cottage on the edge of the village, alone except for a friendly black cat called Duncan.

He preferred to spend most of his time around children, recognising that they possess a sense of wonder at the world which is usually lost by adulthood. He loved the way children constantly question their surroundings and derive pleasure and joy out of the smallest and most mundane of things, such as an empty cardboard box or an unusual wild creature.

The more time Harold spent around the children of the community, the more he appreciated how magical the world was. His interest in them was entirely innocent, and every day he did his best to increase the sum total of wonder and joy and love and delight in the lives of all the children he knew. They, in turn loved Mr Lamb and always enjoyed any chance encounter they had with him, particularly if he was accompanied by Duncan. This was because he invariably showed them a magic trick, which usually involved a pack of cards or a toy rabbit that popped out of one of his pockets. He performed some unusual and impressive tricks with a blend of charisma, comedy, illusion and 'magic' in a remarkable, improvisational style. In fact, the tricks were more than unusual – they were truly awesome.

However, during the last few years of his long and eventful life, Harold would perform his magic only for children, and never in the presence of adults. This was because he had grown resentful of the cynicism and dismissive attitude with which the adults of the village treated his eccentric brand of showmanship. They saw him as a slightly strange, unconventional old man whom they patronised and tolerated with a large degree of superciliousness

And Harold Lamb knew it. He was deeply hurt by the villagers' condescending treatment of him and their obvious cynicism towards his ability and skill as a magician and an illusionist. His resentment was compounded by the belief that the villagers simply didn't understand or care about his desire simply to bring happiness to the local children and suspected his interest in them of being unhealthy, an idea which outraged him. His motive was not to become famous or make any money from his little performances. In his heart of hearts he hoped that everyone had some magic about them, but he felt that all adults had sadly lost their sense of magic and wonderment. It angered him that people cared so little for all the wonderful magic of the world, and that the world at large seemed not to care for, nor appreciate, its own magic.

As a natural-born performer, Harold firmly believed that it was his mission to spread his magic around, because he simply couldn't stop performing it — at least, for the youngsters. After all, magic is so much fun, so beautiful, so true.

In the sincere belief that his magic act would impress even the most fuddy-duddy of adults, if only they would give it a chance, and with the opportunity to entertain the children, he had, over many years, offered to perform free of charge for the village fete, birthday parties, local fundraising and charity events. But all his efforts had been to no avail, for despite the eager pleas of several of the children, the adults of the village had proved completely indifferent to his offers. Denied the opportunity of realising his goals and dreams, Harold found the resultant distress and frustration too much to bear. In old age he grew increasingly bitter, and finally died, they said, of a broken heart.

Harold's body was placed in the local undertaker's chapel of rest whilst arrangements were made for the burial. But on the morning of the funeral, when the undertaker went to secure the lid of the coffin, he was profoundly shocked to find it empty.

Meanwhile on the other side of the village, Seth Garbutt, the local gravedigger, was in for an even greater shock. He returned from his lunch to see Mr Lamb's black cat sitting serenely on top of the pile of earth he had just excavated, and looking down into the newly-dug grave Seth had prepared for the funeral that afternoon. The wretched creature almost seemed to be smiling. How could the cat have known the grave was for its owner?

Seth nearly died of shock when he looked into the hole he had just dug, because Mr Lamb was already in it. Dressed in his Sunday best, the old man was lying peacefully on the fresh earth, quite dead, his hands clasped together over his chest and a contented smile on his features.

His expression said it all. This would teach those smug old villagers whether his magic was a load of nonsense or not.

LIKE FATHER, LIKE SON

The only thing George Badham didn't like about the care home in which his mother was a resident was that it was in a crowded suburban district. He would have preferred it to have been in a rural setting so that she could enjoy pastoral views, fresh air and tranquillity, but he knew that neither he nor the remnants of his mother's dwindling estate could cover the high fees such places demanded. He comforted himself in the knowledge that he had been a dutiful son over the last couple of years, for he and his wife Eileen had visited his mother every week without fail.

It was while he was on his way to see his mother that George had to stop at a red traffic light on an intersection about a mile from his destination. Impatient to get on his way, he was strumming his fingers on the steering wheel when he suddenly felt a chill, as though a shadow had fallen over him. He tried to shrug it off, but he became increasingly convinced that he was being watched. He instinctively looked around, but could see no vehicles or pedestrians. His attention was captured by a large billboard on the far side of the road, bearing a placard the like of which he had never seen before. It was a large, colourful poster for the recruitment of military personnel, and across the top appeared the words: *There is still a place in the line for you - will you fill it?* Underneath these words, a row of uniformed soldiers stood smartly to attention in a cratered, barren landscape. In recognition of their senior officer, the heads of all the soldiers faced to the right except for one member of the group. The soldier standing at the very centre of the row was looking instead directly at George. His outstretched arm seemed to be pointing directly at him, apparently ignoring Eileen, who was sitting beside her husband, wondering what on earth had distracted him.

Puzzled at what he saw on the poster and confused by the fact that there were no vacant places in the row as suggested by the headline, George looked more closely at the image of the soldier at its centre, who seemed familiar. With a shock, he realised that the man appeared to be George's own double.

Telling himself the illusion had to be merely the product of his over-active imagination, George turned his attention back to the road and drove away. Yet somehow he felt that the eyes on the billboard were following him down the road, watching his every move until he disappeared from view.

George did not explain the incident to his wife, and he soon forgot all about it, as over the next few days they had the enjoyable distraction of a short break in their favourite seaside resort. However, during the next weekly visit to see his mother, George found himself stationary at the same traffic lights once again, and despite a feeling of intense trepidation he again forced himself to look at the billboard. It still bore the same poster, with the same words: *There is still a place in the line for you - will you fill it?* He looked at the row of soldiers' faces, and once again recognised his own face. But this time tears appeared to be streaming down the image of his double's face and the soldiers stood not in a cratered, barren landscape but in a field of red flowers which were blowing gently in the breeze – a field of poppies.

This time George did not feel alarmed by what he saw; he was neither shocked, afraid nor confused. He was simply consumed by an overwhelming feeling of sadness, comforted by warm, gentle memories of his early life.

When he eventually reached the care home, George was, for some reason, not at all shocked to learn that his mother had passed away just an hour before his arrival.

Two weeks after her funeral, he made the journey one last time, to thank the staff at the care home for the compassion and tenderness with which they had cared for his mother. The familiar billboard with the words: *There is still a place in the line for you - will you fill it?* still stood near the traffic lights, but the soldier who had been at the centre of the row was missing and there was now indeed a 'place in the line'.

That evening George and Eileen reminisced over an old album of family photographs which contained images of his late mother. Sadly, none of the photographs included his father, who had been killed whilst serving in the armed forces in France during the Second World War shortly before the birth of his son. If he had been able to see a picture of his father, George would quickly have realised that he was his spitting image.

THE WAY TO A MAN'S HEART

Rose Macdonald was a gentle, modest and reserved person. She coped well with most aspects of her everyday life, liked her privacy and was interested in everything that was new or previously unknown to her. Thanks to her quiet, optimistic nature, other people felt relaxed and cheerful in her company, and her personality was characterised by tolerance, a regard for others and an insatiable drive to raise funds for charitable causes, particularly those involving children or the disabled.

Rose was caring and generous, always willing to help anyone in trouble and always full of the milk of human kindness; except, that is, when it came to her narcissistic husband, Gordon, whom she loathed with a passion. She found herself at a loss to understand why she had agreed to marry him. They had wed thirty years previously, six months after they had met at the local hospital where Rose still worked. Gordon had seemed charming enough at first, but he soon turned out to be unpleasantly arrogant, rude, domineering and tyrannical, and he always took the opportunity to make her feel small and embarrass her in the presence of others. She found his constant lying to be very irritating, and frequently felt threatened by his sudden, temperamental mood changes.

Despite his failings, as a dutiful wife Rose did her best to make her husband happy by administering to his every need, but it was all to no avail. The only thing he seemed remotely satisfied with was her cooking, so she spent an inordinate amount of time preparing his favourite dishes. He had a particular penchant for her home-made pies, whether they were filled with fish, cheese and potato, steak with liver and kidney, vegetables, egg and mushroom, blackberry, apple, cherry or a variety of other tasty combinations.

As the years passed, Gordon's behaviour grew even worse. He took increasingly to the bottle, to the point where he became an alcoholic. A concerned hospital doctor warned him that his liver was already showing the signs of excessive drinking, and advised him to stop. Gordon dismissed the diagnosis. No jumped-up little doctor half his age was going to tell him what he could drink and what he couldn't.

The drinking got worse, and the demands Gordon

made on Rose were now becoming so intolerable that she seriously considered leaving him to set up home on her own. But that would have been a huge step. She knew that he would eventually find her, force her to go back to him and make her life even more unbearable. So she continued to pamper to his uncompromising demands and to try to be a good wife, to such an extent that she was frequently utterly exhausted.

Things came to a head in the week leading up to Christmas. Rose had been planning a shopping trip for herself and Edith, a severely disabled friend who rarely had the opportunity to venture outdoors. Throughout the year, Rose had meticulously saved every penny she could in a ceramic money box which she kept at the side of her bed. By the middle of December she calculated that she had enough in the box to pay for bus fares and a nice lunch, which she hoped would bring some joy to her friend on their day out.

On the evening before the much-anticipated day, Rose walked into the bedroom to see that the carpet was covered with shards of smashed pottery; the remains of her money box. Her callous brute of a husband had smashed the box and taken the contents. When he finally returned home the next morning, it became clear that he had spent the money on a long session of binge drinking and gambling. Rose's frustration and anger were compounded when she learnt that earlier in the day Gordon had ridiculed her disabled friend in front of their mutual colleagues at the hospital.

Of course, Gordon did not apologise; he didn't even mention the money. Clearly he took the attitude that what was his was his, and what was his wife's was also his.

Rose spent the day screwing up her courage to challenge him over the money box, but she decided, at the last minute, that she would not mention it. There was no point. It would only lead to insults and possible violence, and the money was gone, never to be recovered.

It was Gordon himself who finally gave Rose her idea. No sooner had he recovered from the drunken stupor than he started setting out his demands for Christmas dinner.

'I don't want any of that turkey crap' he told her. 'Make me a pie. A good big steak, liver and kidney pie.'

Steak, liver and kidney pies were one of his Rose's specialities. Usually she obtained the meat from Mr Merritt, her local butcher, insisting on only the best, because if Gordon came across a piece of fat or gristle he was quite capable of spitting it out on to the table and treating Rose to a stream of invective. But now she had a slightly different plan in mind.

On Christmas Eve, having returned from her last shift at the hospital before the Christmas break, Rose prepared a large steak, liver and kidney pie for her husband, using a slightly different recipe from the usual one, and served it up to him with his favourite creamed potatoes and Brussels sprouts. Gordon ate it without thanks and in silence. It was clear from the speed at which the pie disappeared that the new recipe was a success. He did comment suspiciously at one point about the slightly unusual flavour, but it didn't stop him from finishing the pie in one sitting and demanding another as soon as possible.

Rose smiled quietly to herself. The change to her recipe had been a success; he would get his wish.

When Rose returned to her job in the hospital mortuary following the Christmas recess, she took with her, concealed in her bag, a supply of resealable plastic bags and a small sharp knife. The steak for Gordon's pies would continue to come from Mr Merritt; the other ingredients, however, had a more unusual provenance. After all, his liver was already cirrhotic. What difference would a little more diseased tissue make?

INNOCENCE

The twins' birth had been traumatic and their mother's ordeal had been extreme. In fact, had it not been for the expertise of the professionals who looked after her, neither she nor her offspring would have survived.

Despite their somewhat precarious introduction to life, the pair were fortunate in being allowed to experience their early existence on their own terms. It seemed that at their birth, a light had been switched on – a light which shone through their young lives, encouraging them to follow their desires in the knowledge that no matter what they did, someone would always take care of them and make sure that everything was all right.

With the innocent, carefree confidence of the young, the two youngsters rejoiced in their freedom to explore the world around them, a world of enchanting, bewitching countryside, blissfully far from the hustle and bustle of more populated communities. They revelled in the joy of living, absorbing the scents and sounds of country life and adapting quickly to the rhythms of nature. Food was available whenever they wanted it, which was often, and their mother was always near at hand. Feeling that they had the whole world to themselves, they quickly realised that there were a myriad things they needed to learn in relation to the signals and messages which nature laid before them.

On each day of their young lives, they ran forth joyfully into the morning light across peaceful pastures, their spirits rising like larks towards a heaven in which the whole of nature seemed to join in a clamour of approval. Their knowledge of the world in their early years was limited to what they could see around them, which was all they wanted to know about. On clear nights they would look at the moon, which held a strange attraction, since it induced them to think not only about what they had already learned but to wonder about what lay beyond, across the hills and woods of home, far away in the great wide world.

The youngsters led idyllic lives, revelling in the excitement each day brought, listening to the murmur of the breeze in the long grass of the great meadows, rambling along hedgerows and copses, finding birds building nests and flowers which became more sweet-smelling with the passage of time. They had a lightness of spirit about them and life ran rich and good. They tumbled about mock-fighting, played hide and seek between the trees and raced around with boundless energy, eventually to lie back blissfully in the soft grass to think about what they were going to do in the days and years ahead and to dream waking dreams. In the long summer evenings they would meander aimlessly beside a magnificent, stately river, bewitched by the songs of larks tilting into the warm breeze.

As one month ran on towards the next, there was a change in the air, with the rustle of leaves and the rich smell of dust kicked up when the wind blew. With the dawn of each new day, magical pink and white light shone through thin veils of mist. The woodland and hedgerows were aflame with rich and warm colours enhanced by the glow of the autumn sun. The twins derived great fun and excitement from trying to catch falling leaves, which seemed to dance with delight in evading capture whilst twigs crackled under their feet and the stumps of colourful mushrooms did their best to trip them up.

Notwithstanding their playful sessions of revelry, their journey towards adulthood was gentle and serene, their high spirits undiminished by the passing of the days. Together they would climb a winding mountain track and gaze dreamily into the distance from the comfort of a green-tufted dell in a field close to the summit. From up there, high on the hill, the whole world seemed subdued and at peace.

And so it was on a crystal-clear late autumn day that the twins gazed down from their hillside retreat and noticed a large, white square thing slowly bouncing and clattering its way along the dusty road up to their field. They were not to know that the square object was in fact a lorry. And they certainly wouldn't have understood the meaning of the words on the side of the lorry: 'Quality Butchers and Meat Purveyors'. After all, they were only lambs.

A PROMISE IS A PROMISE

'Hi-Yo, Silver! Away!' came the distinctive cry through the still, cool air of a fine autumn day. Mr Crombie pulled his dog Arthur closer to his side and commanded him to sit, but Arthur merely pricked up his ears in anticipation of whatever was about to unfold.

As the two watched, a young boy appeared in front of Mr Crombie, silhouetted against the iridescent sparkle of light from the late afternoon sun. 'Howdy pardner,' he said cheerfully. Mr Crombie reckoned he was no more than eight years old, judging by his size and the sound of his voice.

The lad was dressed head to toe as the Lone Ranger and wore a black domino mask which covered most of his face. He also wore a grey, long-sleeved cotton shirt buttoned up to the neck, sturdy grey canvas trousers supported by a silver-buckled black belt with black gun holsters and knee-high black leather boots which bore fancy silver spurs. All this was complemented by fringed black gloves, a wide-brimmed white hat which had a tall rounded crown held on by a long leather strap and a large red silk bandanna. He had certainly gone to some trouble to look the part.

The boy was not, however, riding a horse, but a white Mustang BMX bike. He clearly regarded the machine as his horse, because as he performed a very impressive wheelie he admonished it by saying, 'Stand still Silver, yer cavortin' critter!' As the machine obediently returned to a horizontal position, its young owner stroked its handlebars by way of reward. Tied behind the saddle of his bike was a bedroll in the form of a canvas-covered blanket. A short-barrelled carbine toy rifle was attached alongside the crossbar, where the tyre pump should have been.

The junior Lone Ranger stood astride his steed on top of a raised, solid heap of industrial spoil composed of steel slag and colliery waste, situated on rough ground used to store wooden props and white ash from a derelict steelworks. Mr Crombie frequently took Arthur for a walk along one of the many lonely paths which traversed this bleak expanse, which was littered with the abandoned ruins of an old industrial complex. Alongside the pitted concrete paths, remnants of rotting wooden railings leant in all directions, like old men struggling against a strong headwind.

For many years the mills and pits had emptied their waste products into the nearby river, which had been turned yellow by the vitriol waste from an old tinplate works. It was a desolate landscape, and one very much defined by decay; widely dispersed corrugated roofing sheets, twisted railway points weathered by the elements, wheelbarrows with no wheels, rusted drums, metal drinking mugs and old steel helmets lay scattered all around, the tokens of a bygone age long since extinct.

Mr Crombie was surprised to see the Lone Ranger in such a place, since in all the years he had walked through the old industrial wasteland he had never seen another living creature, except for the occasional fox or rabbit which always ran off as soon as they were spotted.

'Where ya headin' with yer buckaroo, Tonto?' asked the Lone Ranger of Mr Crombie.

'We're gonna mosey down to the rodeo,' replied Mr Crombie, in an attempt to humour the youngster. 'You out here in the badlands all on your own son? It's not a very safe place to play you know. Does your mother know you're out here?'

The Lone Ranger ignored Mr Crombie's cross-examination, performed another wheelie and retaliated by forcibly stating, 'Injuns don't go to rodeos on their own, mister. C'mon, we got some pesky outlaws to sort out.'

'Not today, Kemosabe,' said Mr Crombie. 'My buckaroo needs his dinner and so do I. Mind how you go, son.'

'Don't go, Tonto!' implored the youngster, dropping the accent. 'I wanna wooden dagger please mister. Can you get me a wooden dagger wiv me name on it?' He fingered the toy rifle and reverted to his cowboy lingo. 'Do as I say or I'm gonna pump ya' full o' lead!'

'Sure I will, son' said Mr Crombie. 'Just as soon as I can find me a nice piece of wood.'

'I hope you're a man of yer word' said the boy suspiciously.

'I never broke a promise in my danged life' said Mr Crombie cheerfully.

The boy rode off happily, and Mr Crombie resumed his walk. The sun had begun to set by the time he reached home. Mrs Crombie already had dinner served and waiting on the table, and she was not in the best of moods.

'You're late!' she snapped.

'Sorry, dear,' replied her husband. 'Went a bit further than usual.'

His wife tut-tutted loudly and muttered something about not being appreciated and being taken for granted. Mr Crombie thought it best not to proffer any further explanation of the reason for his lateness; his wife was not likely to be impressed to hear that he had been held up by the Lone Ranger. Not that there was much he could do about his promise – the boy hadn't told him his name. He resolved to ask him the next time he saw him.

The golden, balmy days of autumn turned to the perpetual grey, rain-lashed days of a dismal winter, which meant there were limited opportunities for Mr Crombie and Arthur to go walking along the well-frequented paths that traversed the faded industrial grandeur of the old steelworks. They did however manage to take a couple of walks during the long weeks of winter, when Mr Crombie managed to gather some fallen pieces of wooden railings, which he took home to dry as fuel for the living-room fire.

He often wondered what had become of the young Lone Ranger and whether Father Christmas had brought him his much-wanted wooden dagger. Not once during his walks during the winter and spring months did he see any sign of the boy on the bike, or of anyone else who was brave enough to meet the challenge of the long walk amongst the windswept derelict piles of rubble which littered the old steelworks.

The only incident of any note occurred during a walk in late May when Arthur suddenly stopped just as they turned for home. He stared intently at something that wasn't there, crouched down low, moved slowly forward as if stalking something invisible, and then abruptly turned tail and tried to make a dash for home.

By the following autumn Mr Crombie had all but forgotten about his Lone Ranger. It was a surprise therefore when during a late afternoon walk in mid-

October, the boy appeared once again. The first thing Mr. Crombie noticed was the sound of laughter, followed by a sense of a presence on the sudden light breeze.

He put down the broken fragments of wooden fencing he had been collecting for firewood, shaded his eyes and looked upwards to see a black silhouette standing garish on a small mound among the wreckage of twisted beams and corrugated sheets. It was the Lone Ranger, a little taller now but still sitting astride his trusted two-wheeled Silver, his face partly masked by the brim of his hat and the red bandanna he was wearing.

'How ya doin' Tonto, did ya have a hog-killin' time at the rodeo?' asked the lad. 'I see yer've gone and brung me ma wooden dagger!'

He was pointing to the pieces of wood on the floor. Mr Crombie noticed that a small two-piece section of the fence did indeed resemble a long-bladed, short-handled dagger in the shape of a cross.

'Has it got ma name on it?' asked the boy.

Much as Mr Crombie wanted to give the youngster the 'dagger' he desired so much, he was concerned that the rough wood of the old fencing could splinter badly and cause him some harm.

'I'm afraid it doesn't have your name on it lad, because you never told me your name. I'm going to take this wood back home for the fire,' apologised Mr Crombie.

He was startled by the cold anger of the boy's reaction.

'Then you broke your promise,' said the young Lone Ranger. 'You're no faithful friend of mine at all.' His quiet, assertive tone of voice took Mr Crombie by surprise.

What happened next surprised him even more. The boy drew the rifle from the crossbar of his machine, levelled it at Mr Crombie and cocked the hammer.

'You win, pardner' said Mr Crombie uneasily. 'Guess I shoulda kept my promise. I could still…'

His words were cut off abruptly. The boy swung the rifle down so that it was pointing at Arthur, sitting obediently by his owner's side. He pressed the gilded trigger, and instead of the harmless crack of a percussion cap, there came a thunderous bang; the sound of a full-bore rifle going off. Arthur collapsed instantly, briefly pumping blood from a hole in his side.

Mr Crombie gaped in shock. The boy holstered the rifle, then reached down and drew a pair of ivory-handled single-action Colt .45 revolvers from the holsters at his belt, one in each gloved hand. He raised the pistols, scowled, steadied his aim at Mr Crombie and fired. The roar of the guns sounded almost simultaneously, and two holes appeared side by side in Mr Crombie's forehead. He stood for a second with an expression of bemusement on what was left of his face, then collapsed across the body of his dog like a felled tree.

A momentary breeze blew up some white industrial ash which settled like powdered snow on the two corpses. A glint of sun revealed the skeletal mouth and teeth of the BMX rider, which until now had been disguised by the red silk bandanna. There was a hint of a lingering, sidelong smile.

In the low slant of early evening light, the Lone Ranger removed one of his gloves and with fleshless, bony fingers picked up his newly-acquired wooden dagger.

'This will do to mark my spot,' he whispered, 'It ain't that much to ask, is it? It's not as if I'm wanted, dead or alive.'

He remounted his metallic steed and rode off through the windswept, derelict landscape until he had reached the mouth of a dark, deep, long forgotten mine shaft. Then he paused wistfully and gently dropped the wooden cross onto the floor. At least he now had something more than a patch of nettles to mark his last resting place.

He performed one last wheelie. 'Hi-Yo, Silver! Away!' he called.

The wind whipped about him as the Lone Ranger rode for the last time down into the black void of the pit.

WITH JACK'S COMPLIMENTS

Old Jack he lived in a box
His hair was made out of flocks
He jumped out one day
With children to play
His face was covered in pox.

Alarmed by spotty old Jack
They boxed the ogre straight back
When the lid came down
On top of the clown
The children heard a loud crack.

Now Jack had broken a flask
And donned a shiny black mask
He bided his time
And planned his next crime
The kids, he'd take them to task.

The flask had stored all the pores
That clad Jack's face with the sores
He spread them about
When next he popped out
Old Jack had settled some scores

THE COLOUR OF DEATH

It was a strange combination; the odour of old, musty brickwork painted in white emulsion mixed with the strong smell of disinfectant used to scrub the floors. It pervaded every corner of the labyrinthine network of corridors which linked the various parts of the old hospital building. A single-storey edifice constructed by prisoners of war, it reeked of history. The grief of the broken hearts of a thousand relatives seemed to weep from the cracks in its white walls, and it was all too easy to imagine the spirits of hundreds of patients who had departed this life shuffling eternally along its endless corridors.

Yet although the place was redolent of the hopelessness of humanity's ignorance in relation to disease and what to do about it, it also carried, in the daytime, the buzz of high professionalism. It was the kind of place which inspired some of those who worked there, even if it brought only tragedy and despair to the relatives and friends of those patients who failed to respond to the devoted and solicitous attentions of the staff.

One of the things Emily enjoyed about working evening shifts was the peace and quiet which permeated the hospital following the hustle and bustle of the customary working day. The more relaxed atmosphere of the evening afforded her an opportunity to familiarise herself with the tasks demanded of her new role as a phlebotomist and to gain some self-confidence in the collection of blood samples. She was proud of her freshly-acquired status and keen to show her line managers in the laboratory that she was competent at her job and could be relied upon to deliver a first-class service, not only to her patients but to her employer and to her profession.

She was perfectly content to be employed by an organisation which she knew could make a real difference to people's lives in an age when the public truly respected those who catered for their health and well-being. She was mildly irritated when wisecracking patients called her a "vampire", but she humoured them by playing along with their hackneyed remarks and would bare her teeth like glistening fangs to show she could take a joke.

One dreary winter's evening as Emily set out on her ward round along the long, lonely corridors, she couldn't help her thoughts drifting to the many departed dead who had travelled this way. Secured on top of a poorly-disguised metal trolley, they were wheeled along these very passageways on their way to the hospital mortuary, either for release to undertakers or to await the gruesome second execution of a statutory post mortem.

The blackness of the night outside was disguised by the overhead fluorescent lights, which, together with the distinctive sound of the hospital's generators, provided Emily with welcome reassurance that she was in the land of the living and a reminder that she was part of a team which could bring at least some success in keeping death at bay. The sound of her shoes flip-flopped on the bleached floor as she strode briskly to the neurosurgery ward which was her first port of call on the hospital wing to which she had been allocated for the evening shift.

'Just as well to get this one over and done with, it should be downhill after this,' muttered Emily.

She was understandably apprehensive about starting her work on this particular ward, since most of the patients were too far gone to communicate even the most basic information. This made it difficult for Emily to be absolutely certain that she was taking blood samples from the correct patient, since they couldn't even confirm their name, let alone their date of birth and home address.

She knocked on the door of the nurse's office as she entered to pick up the blood sample requests left for her by the medical staff. She wasn't particularly surprised to find that there was no one in the office and correctly surmised that the nurses were accompanying the doctors on their routine evening ward round. She picked up the request forms left for her on the desk and made her way down the ward to her first patient, who was in such a critical state that he had been isolated in one of the side cubicles. Emily knew which cubicle to make for, since one of the nurses had written a large 'NUMBER 8' at the top of the specific request form, a practice adopted by the ward staff to help their hospital colleagues in locating individual patients. However, in keeping with the strict protocol dictated by the hospital's policy on the accurate verification of a patient's true identity, she still needed to be certain for herself that this was indeed the correct patient.

She slid open the concertina door of cubicle number 8. According to the request form, the patient's name was Simon Gregory Armstrong, but a quick glance at the patient, whose antiquated face resembled that of a demonic doll, was enough to dismiss any hopes that he might be able to confirm his name or any other information. He was propped up in his bed, eyes closed and sunken in his gaunt face, bare chested, with the bedclothes tucked around his midriff. His tongue hung from his mouth with the looseness of old age.

She began by asking the patient his name as she was

required to do, just in case he could provide her with the answer, but there was no response, as expected. In keeping with protocol she proceeded to verify his identity by checking the details on his wristband. This pale lilac-coloured plastic strap bore all the relevant information Emily needed to feel satisfied that she was indeed taking blood from the correct patient. She tied her tourniquet around his right arm just above the elbow, swabbed the area of skin around the most prominent vein on his forearm and punctured the vein with a fresh needle attached to a large syringe. She kept at it for several minutes, but despite her best endeavours she failed to extract a trace of blood.

This was not such an unusual occurrence, because even the most skilled and experienced phlebotomists sometimes fail to draw a single drop of blood from the most prominent of veins. Nevertheless, Emily was determined to succeed in leeching the moribund Mr Armstrong of the blood samples that she was tasked to take back to the lab. She tied the tourniquet as tight as she judged was appropriate and tried several times, in different veins on the same arm, but all was to no avail.

She was just leaning down to try one last time when she had the shock of her life. The patient spoke.

'Try the other arm, love,' murmured Mr Armstrong. 'I've been here a few times, everyone seems to have trouble with this arm. They seem to do better with the other one.'

This startled Emily to such an extent that she had to sit on the bed to recover. She had convinced herself that the figure lying before her was comatose. The vacant, glassy look in his pale blue eyes as he gazed blankly at Emily seemed to suggest that this indeed had been the case. It was hard to believe that speech had just emerged from those desiccated lips.

Mr Armstrong's eyes suddenly closed again and he reverted to his former state, completely unresponsive to any of Emily's appeals for him to straighten his left arm and clench his fist to induce the veins in his forearm to become more pronounced. Despite several valiant attempts at drawing blood from both arms, she had to admit defeat.

She decided to leave the peculiar Mr Armstrong in peace for a moment and move on to the other patients on the ward, and having successfully collected blood samples from them all, despite the fact that many had difficult veins or were uncooperative, either through their state of health or age, she felt her self-confidence recovering.

On her way out, she popped into the nurses' office to tell them she had failed to take any samples from Mr Armstrong and to leave the request forms for the medics, in the hope that they would have more success. She was heartened to find that the senior nurse on duty that evening was her long-standing friend Graham Watkins, known to one and all as Bunny.

'What's up, Bunny?' asked Emily, 'haven't seen you in ages.'

'Watcha Ems, nice to see you again,' replied Bunny. 'What's up? you look like you've seen a ghost.'

'I've had a problem with Mr Armstrong in number 8, I'm afraid. I've tried and tried, but I can't get a drop out of him. Can you ask one of the medics to have a go?'

'What, Mr Armstrong? You 'aven't been sticking needles in him have you? I'm not surprised you can't get blood out of him, he's been dead since lunchtime. We haven't had time to sort him out yet 'cause of the ward round.'

Emily gasped. 'You can't be serious!'

'Only too serious. I wish I was joking, but I ain't. If you've been sticking needles in him I'm afraid we'll need to write up a report. Officially, it's the desecration of a deceased person. Didn't yer see the lilac band round his wrist? We only put those on dead 'uns. Those who are alive have white ones. Lilac's the colour that stands for the link between the spiritual and the physical worlds, you know. It's associated with the transformation of the soul.'

Emily's legs began to give way. She felt faint.

Bunny's smile faded. 'Here, sit down, have a glass of water' he said, concerned. 'It's not that bad, just procedure, you'll be all right. Here, you're as white as a sheet.'

Emily slumped into the offered chair in shock.

'But he spoke to me!' she said.

'I don't think so' said Bunny. 'Perhaps it was just air escaping from his lungs, it can sound like they're talkin'.'

'No, he spoke really clearly' she protested. 'He said "Try the other arm, love". He told me he'd been here before.'

'Not in this life he ain't. Look, I'll get the doctor on call, he'll reassure you' said Bunny.

The on-call doctor was concerned at Emily's story, but he clearly did not believe a word of it. According to him, Mr Armstrong had been certified dead over some hours before Emily had got to him.

It was almost midnight by the time the official paperwork had been completed in relation to the 'incident involving the desecration of a deceased person' and Emily had finally returned to the lab to report the unfortunate events of the evening to her line manager. Recognising that she was in a troubled state of mind, her manager reassured her that it could have happened to any of her colleagues. He advised her to go home and invited her to take some sick leave the following day in order to recover from her shock.

By the time Emily had collected her personal belongings from the staffroom, the last bus of the day had long gone. She made her way to the A&E Department to use the dedicated phone line there to summon a taxi to take her home. A taxi pulled up outside the Department within moments, and she clambered in, exhausted.

As the cab rumbled along the deserted urban streets, Emily could not stop thinking about the events of the evening. She found herself going over them again and again. It just didn't make sense, and yet surely she could not have been imagining it. The old man had spoken so clearly. He had looked dead, but he couldn't have been – he just couldn't. And what on earth did he mean by saying he'd 'been here before'?

She was alarmed to notice that the taxi had suddenly begun to accelerate. She looked out of the window at the trees and bushes charging past in the dark; they could be nowhere near her home. In fact they appeared to be travelling at high speed down a narrow country lane.

'What's going on? Where are you going?' she asked. In reply the man raised his hand to turn on the internal light and held up his wrist for Emily to see.

Around it was a pale lilac label. Emily gasped in horror.

The driver's eyes grinned at her in the rear-view mirror. 'They put it on me in the hospital earlier' he said. 'But you didn't notice the colour, did you, eh? And I'll tell you what, you're going to need one just like it, very soon.'

In the dim light from the ceiling of the cab, she could now make out his face. It appeared to be none other than the late Mr Armstrong.

And now the headlights of an oncoming lorry were bearing down on them at terrifying speed.

'Stop! Let me out!' screamed Emily.

But this time the driver did not reply. Instead he simply put his foot down, and the car hurtled on towards oblivion.